D1466548

AMONG THE FREE

Also by Margaret Peterson Haddix

The Missing series

Book 1: *Found*

Book 2: *Sent*

Book 3: *Sabotaged*

The Shadow Children series

Among the Hidden

Among the Impostors

Among the Betrayed

Among the Barons

Among the Brave

Among the Enemy

The Girl with 500 Middle Names

Because of Anya

Say What?

Dexter the Tough

Running Out of Time

The House on the Gulf

Double Identity

Don't You Dare Read This, Mrs. Dunphrey

Leaving Fishers

Just Ella

Turnabout

Takeoffs and Landings

Escape from Memory

Uprising

Palace of Mirrors

AMONG THE FREE

MARGARET PETERSON
HADDIX

Simon & Schuster Books for Young Readers
New York London Toronto Sydney

SIMON & SCHUSTER BOOKS FOR YOUNG READERS
An imprint of Simon & Schuster Children's Publishing Division
1230 Avenue of the Americas, New York, New York 10020

For information about special discounts for bulk purchases, please contact Simon & Schuster Special Sales at 1-866-506-1949 or business@simonandschuster.com.
The Simon & Schuster Speakers Bureau can bring authors to your live event. For more information or to book an event, contact the Simon & Schuster Speakers Bureau at 1-866-248-3049 or visit our website at www.simonspeakers.com.
Also available in a hardcover edition.
Book design by Greg Stadnyk
The text for this book is set in Elysium.
Manufactured in the United States of America
0912OFF
First paperback edition July 2007
10
The Library of Congress has cataloged the hardcover edition as follows:
Haddix, Margaret Peterson.
Among the free / Margaret Peterson Haddix.—1st ed.
p.cm.—(A Shadow Children book)
Summary: When thirteen-year-old Luke Garner unwittingly sets off a rebellion which sweeps the country and ousts the Population Police from power, he quickly realizes that the new regime is corrupt and he may hold the only key to true freedom.
ISBN 978-0-689-85798-0 (hc)
[1. Freedom—Fiction. 2. Conduct of life—Fiction. 3. Science fiction.]
I. Title. II. Series.
PZ7H1164Alf 2006
[Fic]—dc22
2005013025
ISBN 978-0-689-85799-7 (pbk)
ISBN 978-1-4169-3445-5 (eBook)

For Doug

ACKNOWLEDGMENTS

With thanks to my agent, Tracey Adams, and editor, David Gale, for their help with and encouragement for the entire Shadow Children series.

AMONG THE FREE

CHAPTER ONE

Luke Garner stood shoulder to shoulder with a dozen other boys, waiting. It was six A.M., time for the daily inspection of all workers at Population Police headquarters, when all their uniforms had to be perfectly fitted, perfectly spotless, perfectly pressed; all their spines perfectly straight; all their expressions perfectly obedient. But Luke and the boys beside him were stablehands, the lowest of the low, so even though they had to line up outside at six A.M., sometimes it was six thirty or even seven before the sergeant stalked down the row. He'd peer at them suspiciously, assigning extra work any time he saw a wayward lock of hair, a wayward crease in a uniform, or even the suspicion of a smirk on a boy's face.

"You!" he'd bark. "Shovel all the manure from stall one into stall two. And then shovel all of that into stall three . . ."

Only the stupidest boy would protest that that method was inefficient and would take twice as long, that his time might be better spent doing some other chore. All the boys in this lineup had learned not to be that stupid. Once, a long time ago, soon after Luke had arrived at Population Police headquarters, a boy had dared to question a task: "Isn't there a bigger shovel I can use? It'd go faster that way." The boy had been beaten in full sight of all the other boys.

And then he'd disappeared.

Luke had not made any friends in the stable. The unspoken rule seemed to be *Keep to yourself.* But Luke spent a lot of time thinking about the boy who had dared to ask a question, the one who'd disappeared.

"Atten-tion!" It was the sergeant, arriving earlier than he ever had before.

"Yes, sir!" Luke shouted back with the other boys, snapping his arm up into a salute. He worried that his arm had come up too late, that his "yes, sir!" had been a split second too slow, that he'd be singled out for punishment. The sergeant narrowed his eyes, seeming to stare straight at Luke, and Luke's heart pounded in his chest. But then the sergeant's gaze fell on the next boy in the line.

"You are worthless stableboys," the sergeant spat out. He glared at each boy in turn. "You're no better than the manure you wallow in."

"Yes, sir!" Luke and the other boys yelled. They'd been trained. They knew what they were supposed to say.

"But . . ." The sergeant paused. This was different. Usually he could go on berating them endlessly. "Some of you will have a chance to better yourselves." A new tone had entered his voice. Slyness? Uncertainty?

For the millionth time since he'd left his home nearly a year earlier, Luke wished he could understand other people better, that he could see through their lies to hear what they were actually saying.

"Some of you will be called to a higher purpose," the sergeant continued. "Some of you will be reassigned to a new task for the glory of our country."

None of the boys dared to move, but Luke could practically feel the others around him wanting to exchange glances, to see if anyone else knew what the sergeant was talking about. Higher purpose? New task? What did that mean?

Another man strode up beside the sergeant. He was taller, more imposing. His uniform was more crisply pressed, and he had a row of medals on his chest.

"I'll choose," he said imperiously.

He walked up and down the row of boys, peering carefully at each one of them. Luke held his breath, as if exhaling might call too much attention to himself. He didn't want to be reassigned. He liked working with the horses. They were . . . safe. The stables were a good place to hide.

I, for one, have had enough of hiding. Words a friend had spoken months ago echoed in his mind. Luke had not come to Population Police headquarters looking for safety; only a fool would want to hide there. Luke and his friends had had plans. They'd had dreams. But they hadn't realized how big Population Police headquarters were, how difficult it would be just to pass a message from one person to another. Luke couldn't be sure he and his friends had accomplished anything. Sometimes when he was brushing down a horse, he'd whisper into the horse's quivering ear, "Maybe I am just a worthless stableboy. Maybe that's okay."

Luke had spent most of his thirteen years around hogs, not horses, and any hog would have looked back at him with its piggy eyes as if to say, *So? You think I care?* But the horses looked at Luke as if they understood. One horse in particular had a way of sliding her nose under Luke's arm as if she were comforting him, as if she wanted to say, *I know you've been through a lot. I know you've been hurt and hungry. I know you miss your family and friends. I know you're scared. You just stay right here with me and you'll be fine.* Secretly, Luke called this horse Jenny, in memory of a friend of his, Jen Talbot. But deep down he knew that the human Jen would not have been so comforting. Jen probably would have screamed at him: *What you are talking about? You're not just some worthless stableboy. You're important! Go out and change the world!*

Luke was starting to feel a little dizzy from not breathing. He dared to ease a little air out of his lungs, to take another shallow breath.

The man with the medals on his chest was taking his time walking down the row of boys, staring into their eyes, reaching out to test their arm muscles.

"You," the man said, picking out the tallest kid in the row and shoving him to the other side of the room. "And you," he said, yanking the most muscular boy out of the line.

Luke allowed himself to take a deeper breath. He let himself notice how cold it was out here in the early morning chill, and think about how much warmer it would be back in the stables. Two down, only one to go—he was probably safe. Of the boys remaining, he wasn't the tallest or the heaviest or the strongest. He was just a typical scrawny kid.

The man narrowed his eyes, examining the boys left in the lineup. He grabbed one boy's head so he could stare into the boy's ears; he studied another boy's straw-colored hair. Luke half expected the man to reach into some boy's mouth to look at his teeth, the way the head groom did with the horses.

Good thing Mrs. Talbot managed to get the braces off my teeth, Luke thought. He had a flash of remembering a lighthearted moment in the midst of sorrow and fear: him and his friends laughing in a cozy cottage while Mrs. Talbot tugged on metal bands and wires and protested, "Look, kids, orthodontia is not my specialty. What do they put these things on with? Cement?" In that moment, Luke hadn't cared that the braces endangered him, linking him to a suspect past. He hadn't even cared that all her tugging and scraping hurt. He'd just been happy to laugh with his friends.

Now something caught in his throat, and he had to swallow hard to fight back his memories, to hold back his sense that he deserved to be—no, that he *was*—more than a worthless, lonely stableboy. Maybe he made a little noise, deep in his throat. The man with the medals on his chest snapped his head toward Luke, focused the gaze of his narrowed eyes squarely on Luke's face. The man gave Luke a cruel, thin-lipped smile. In horror, Luke watched the man slowly lift his arm—higher, higher, and higher, until it was aimed straight out from his body, the first finger extended.

"You," the man said.

He was pointing at Luke.

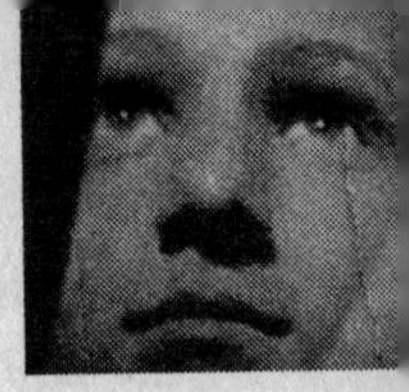

CHAPTER TWO

Luke sat numbly in the backseat of a huge van. He'd been given no explanation of where he was going, no chance to gather up his belongings or to say good-bye to anyone. Luke wasn't sure he wanted to know where he was going, and he had no belongings to speak of anyhow. But as the car passed out of the gates of Population Police headquarters, he had to bite back a scream: *No, wait—stop! I have to talk to Nina and Trey and Nedley and Matthias. And, oh, Mark—my brother—I don't even know if he's here! Please! I have to tell them—*

The van zoomed on, and Luke kept silent. It wasn't safe even to speak his friends' names. It wasn't safe to reveal that he knew them, that he'd ever had a life beyond shoveling manure for the Population Police.

"What's wrong with you?" the boy beside Luke asked. Luke realized that he'd been wincing, that he'd failed to hide his anguish completely.

"I, uh—I'm going to miss the horses," Luke said.

"Why? You still have their stink on you," the boy said, and laughed rudely. He scooted away from Luke, closer to the boy on the other side of him, who laughed too. Luke heard them whispering about "stable rats."

And then Luke really did miss the horses, particularly Jenny with her comforting gaze.

What am I going to do? Luke wondered. *Nina and the others won't know what happened to me. What if they think I've chickened out and run away? What if they're counting on me for one of our plans, and I'm not there? What if the plan is ruined because of that and someone gets hurt or killed or—discovered?*

So many of their plans had gone wrong already. Luke and his friends had been terrified just stepping foot in Population Police headquarters. The Population Police had been created more than a dozen years ago, after a series of droughts and famines had made many people fear that their entire country would starve. The Government made it illegal for any family to have more than two children, and it was the job of the Population Police to hunt down and kill third children.

Luke was a third child. So were Nina and Trey and Matthias . . . all his friends.

Jen had been a third child too, but she'd been so brave and foolhardy that she'd organized a rally to ask for rights and freedom. She'd died at that rally. It had happened ten months ago, but the more time passed, the worse Luke felt about it.

That was just one of the reasons he felt capable of little more than shoveling manure.

If anyone can defeat the Population Police, it's us. The words flickered in Luke's mind like a lightbulb about to go out. That was what Trey had said back in the fall, persuading everyone to go to Population Police headquarters to try to sabotage the group from within. Trey was the smartest kid Luke knew. Why hadn't he seen how that sentence could be flipped around?

If we can't defeat the Population Police, nobody can.

Luke and his friends had tried to destroy certain Population Police documents, but there had been copies they hadn't known about. They'd tried to protect rebels who were making fake identity cards for illegal third children, but the Population Police had killed the rebels anyway. They'd tried to pass out stockpiled food to starving people, but the Population Police had gotten it all back.

If we can't defeat the Population Police . . . Truly hopeless words seemed to push their way into his mind: *Why bother?*

Luke closed his eyes and leaned his head against the cool glass of the window. And then he surrendered himself to sleep.

When he woke up, the van was stopped and the man with the medals on his chest was yelling at all the boys to get out and stand at attention.

"We're here! No time to waste! Out! Out, you lazy dogs!"

Luke was used to being yelled at, because of the stables. He knew that yells were quickly followed by swats and boxed ears and beatings if he didn't obey instantly. He stumbled through the van door before he'd even glanced outside. An icy wind pushed at him the minute he landed on the ground; mud sucked at his boots and made walking difficult. But he lined up and snapped his arm into attention position. Only then did he dare to look around, letting his eyes dart from side to side.

They were parked before a long, low building, seemingly in the middle of nowhere, surrounded by nothing but mud. No—there was more: A lineup of jeeps, more than Luke had ever seen before, stood idling just beyond the building. Uniformed men came rushing out of the building toward the vehicles. The man with the medals started counting off boys and shoving them in the direction of the jeeps.

"You two, go with Officer Ludwick. Over there. You two, with Officer Straley. You two—" The man pounded Luke's back, almost knocking him to the ground. Between the wind and his struggle to keep from falling, Luke barely heard the man's orders. Did he say Luke was supposed to go with Officer Hook? Or was it Officer Hawk? He hoped the other boy with him—the one who'd said Luke smelled like horse manure—had been paying attention. Luke scrambled off behind everyone else.

The mud still tugged at his boots, almost pulling one off. A memory flashed through his mind from childhood: Luke and his brothers running barefoot through mud. Barefoot was so much easier, but Mother always made them spray off their feet before they came into the house. . . .

And then Luke shut that memory off, slamming a door in his mind. He couldn't think about Mother or his brothers right now. He just had to concentrate on reaching the proper jeep, sliding in, pulling his feet away from the ground before the jeep leaped forward.

"Officer Houk signing out, jeep serial number 80256," said one of the men in the front seat. He was speaking into a small phonelike object, maybe a walkie-talkie or some other kind of two-way radio. "With one driver and"—he glanced at Luke and the other boy in the backseat—"two assistants. Bound for Chiutza. Over."

"Copy that. Mission approved," a voice crackled out of the radio.

Chiutza? Luke thought. *Is that a place?* He'd never heard of it, but there was so much he'd never heard of before. He'd never even stepped foot off his parents' farm until he was twelve years old. His parents hadn't liked to discuss things beyond the edges of their property.

"Why talk of things that only make us sad?" Luke's mother had explained once, tears glistening in her eyes.

Luke couldn't remember what he'd asked her that particular day. He could remember asking only once about why he'd had to hide, why the Government thought it was wrong for him to be alive, why he couldn't go around freely like his brothers did. He wished now that he'd asked lots of questions: *What did you think my life would be worth, hiding like that? What did you think would become of me? Why didn't you and all your friends and neighbors and the rest of the country do something to stop the Government, way back in the beginning? What would you do if you were in a speeding jeep and everyone thought you were on the Population Police's side and you had to pretend to be, but really—*

"Here." The man holding the radio surprised Luke by tossing something into the backseat. "We've got at least an hour before we get there. Eat."

Luke started to reach for the packet that landed between him and the other boy, but the other boy grabbed it first. The boy peeled back greasy paper to reveal two hunks of cornbread, which he instantly crammed into his mouth in one bite. He chewed with his mouth open, leering at Luke and dropping crumbs on the seat.

"But—" The wind carried away Luke's protest. Luke clamped his teeth together, swallowing everything he wanted to say.

"You'll need your energy in Chiutza," Officer Houk said from the front seat. *Now* he turned around, now that all evidence of the other boy's greed was out of sight. "You have to knock on every door and summon every resident to a meeting in the town square."

"Why?" It was the other boy who asked this. Stealing Luke's food must have made him cocky.

Luke flinched, waiting for Officer Houk to reach back and strike the boy, and maybe Luke, too, for good measure. But Officer Houk only frowned.

"We're issuing new identification cards to every citizen in the country," Officer Houk said. "We're doing it all at once, in a single day. That's where all these jeeps are going, to give out the I.D.'s in other towns and villages." He gestured at the vehicles ahead of them and behind them, some already turning off the main road to smaller, rutted paths.

Luke knew better than to ask the next question. He knew about officers' tempers. But he couldn't stop the words bursting out of his own mouth: "Why do people need new I.D.'s? What's wrong with the old ones?"

Officer Houk narrowed his eyes at Luke, studying Luke's face. *He really sees me now. He'll remember me,* Luke thought, fighting the familiar terror that had haunted him ever since he'd come out of hiding, the familiar desire to scream, *Don't look at me!* Luke didn't even bother to brace himself to be hit, because it didn't matter. No punishment was worse than being stared at.

But Officer Houk only shrugged.

"There's nothing wrong with the old I.D.'s," he said. "The new ones are just better."

And Luke, who had to fight so hard to read facial expressions, who had to struggle to interpret tones in strangers' voices, watched carefully as Officer Houk turned back around to face the wind rushing at them.

He's lying, Luke thought, hopefully. Then, with less certainty: *If he's lying, I think I know the truth. Could it be—?*

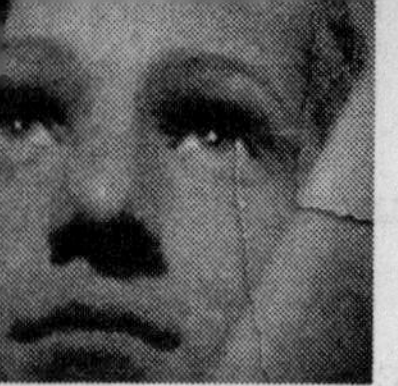

CHAPTER THREE

It had been one of their riskiest plans. At Population Police headquarters, Luke and his friends had heard rumors that the leaders were collecting identity cards for some big test, to sort out legal citizens and illegal third children once and for all.

"They're all in one spot," Nina had whispered in Luke's ear once when she'd brought food out to the stable. Nina worked in the headquarters kitchen; she was the only one of his friends that Luke ever saw. That day he'd blinked stupidly at her, not quite understanding until she hissed, "We can destroy them."

Then Luke had wanted to ask, *How?* and *What good would that do?* and *What if it's all a trap?* and *What makes you think we have any prayer of succeeding?* But Nina had stepped back quickly, gathering up serving trays, so he'd had no time to say anything after she told him what to do.

Luke's assignment had been to place a particularly pungent glob of horse manure in the middle of a path, in order to delay an officer who was rushing to repair a security fence. Luke had taken the manure from Jenny's stall; he'd arranged it carefully to look fresh and accidental and unplanned. After that he'd heard nothing more about I.D.'s, nothing more about the plan.

He thought it must have failed. Failed, like every other plan.

But if they're issuing new I.D.'s to everyone in the country, maybe the old ones really were destroyed. Maybe . . .

Maybe it didn't matter. And even if it did, how could Luke take any pride in the plan's success when all he had done was arrange horse manure?

Luke shivered in the bitter wind pushing its way into the jeep. The bleak countryside flashed past him: leafless trees and lifeless fields.

"My dad had a mechanic's shop, back home," the other boy said suddenly. "I'm good with cars."

Luke forced himself to turn and look at the other boy.

"Yeah?" Luke said. Did this kid actually think Luke would want to be friendly with someone who'd stolen his bread?

"Yeah," the boy said. "So it was stupid that they had me polishing shoes at Population Police headquarters."

He said this softly, as if he didn't want the officer and the driver in the front to hear.

Luke shrugged.

"What did you expect?"

The boy got a dreamy look on his face that softened all his features.

"Food," he said. "I just wanted to eat. To have a full stomach for once in my life. Isn't that why everyone joined up?"

Luke shrugged again, and went back to staring out at the dead landscape. He knew that the Population Police had control of the entire country's food supply; he knew that every family had to have someone working for the Population Police or they'd get no food. But he still felt like yelling at the boy, *The Population Police kill children, don't you know that? Do you even care? Is your full stomach worth other kids' lives?*

Luke and the other boy were silent for the rest of the drive. The men in the front seat didn't seem to be talking to each other either, but Officer Houk kept holding the radio to his mouth and muttering, "Seeking report on identification process in Searcy," or, "What's the progress in Ryana?" Luke wondered vaguely if he was in charge of other units as well, or if he was just nosy.

Then the ruts and potholes in the road grew so huge that Officer Houk put his radio down and concentrated on telling the driver which way to go: "Ease it out gradually—oof! That just caught the right rear tire. You don't think the axle's bent, do you?" Twice Luke and the other boy had to get out and push. Luke thought he heard the other boy muttering, "Stupid, stupid, stupid. This is no way to treat a motor vehicle." But Luke made no attempt to catch the boy's eye or to exchange "at least we're in this together" shrugs.

When they finally reached Chiutza, hours later, Luke was sweating despite the cold, and his bones were jarred from so much bouncing.

"Quickly," Officer Houk ordered, hurrying everyone out of the jeep. "Get everyone in the town square by"—he glanced at his watch—"eleven o'clock. Each of you take one street then report back and I'll assign the next one."

"Street" was too fancy a word for the trash-strewn paths lying before them. Luke could tell that once upon a time, years and years and years ago, Chiutza had had nicely paved streets and concrete sidewalks and sturdy houses. Now the streets were more gravel than pavement, the sidewalks fell off into gaping holes, and the houses were ramshackle, with doors hanging loose and windows patched with plastic.

"Stop gawking and go!" Officer Houk shouted.

Luke saw that the driver and the other boy were scurrying to the right and straight ahead, so Luke veered to the left. The first house he came to looked somehow sadder than all the rest, because it had clearly once been quite grand. It had two stories while most of the others had only one, and it was surrounded by a painted fence, now broken down in decay.

Don't look, Luke told himself.

He pushed aside a cracked gate and went to pound on the front door.

"Open up! Population Police!" he shouted.

And then he shivered, because who was he to be yelling those words? He remembered his brother Mark playing cruel tricks on him when he was a child, pretending Luke's worst nightmares had come true. He remembered a time he'd heard those words from the inside of a house, when he'd had to hide to save his life.

And he remembered another time, when he'd been caught and carried away. . . .

Desperately, Luke shoved himself against the door, as if he could escape his own memories. The door gave way, rusty hinges tearing away from rotting wood. Luke stumbled into a dim living room and found an old woman sitting on a faded couch. Sitting there knitting, as if she'd had no intention of answering the door.

Luke stared at her and she stared at him. Then she said, almost mildly, "It wasn't locked. You didn't have to break it down."

The light caught in the woman's glasses, which threw off slivers of color, like a prism. A cloud of white hair swirled around her face, making her seem unearthly. She looked frail without seeming delicate or feeble. Luke found himself wondering if this was what his own grandmother looked like—the grandmother who'd never even been allowed to know of Luke's existence.

"The Population Police require your attendance at a meeting at eleven o'clock in the town square. You will be issued a new identity card. No other cards or papers will be valid after these cards are issued," Luke said in a rush. And then he turned to go, because he didn't want to think about how he'd broken the woman's door, how he was acting like a typical, brutish Population Police recruit, how this woman's eyes seemed to accuse him. But even as he turned, Luke could see that the woman was making no effort to rise from her couch.

"This is mandatory," he said, still moving toward the door.

"No," the woman said.

Luke stopped, certain he'd heard wrong.

"What?" he said.

"I said no," the woman said calmly. "I'm not going."

"Don't you know what 'mandatory' means?" Luke demanded. "You have to go!"

"No," the woman said again. "I have a choice. You can call it mandatory. You can call it required. But I can make up my own mind. And I'm not going."

Luke heard footsteps outside.

"What's going on in there? Why is this taking so long?" Officer Houk screamed.

Luke could hear him shoving the door, which then fell away completely from the frame, slamming to the floor. Luke jumped out of the way, but not before the door hit his leg.

Officer Houk glanced at the door on the floor, then glared at the woman.

"Come along," he growled.

"She says—," Luke started to explain, but then he felt like he was tattling.

"I'll speak for myself," the woman said. "I am through cooperating with the Population Police. You said if we followed your rules, obeyed your laws, we'd have peace and prosperity. Is this peace—men breaking into my house for no reason? Is this prosperity?" She gestured broadly at her house and yard, and Luke saw that her dress was held together with safety pins. "You said that if my son went off to work for you, we'd all have food. Now my son is gone, and I'm still starving. And you really think I care about identity cards?"

Officer Houk reached down for something on his belt. A gun, Luke realized in horror. Officer Houk pointed it at the woman and said through gritted teeth, "You—will—obey."

"No," the woman said once again, her voice steady, almost joyful.

Officer Houk lowered his gun.

CHAPTER FOUR

Luke stared in amazement. Could it really be that easy? Tell the Population Police no—and they back down? Had anyone else ever thought to try that approach?

But Officer Houk wasn't backing down.

"I'm not wasting a bullet shooting her here, where no one else can see," he said. "Carry her out to the town square and I'll execute her there. Where all of Chiutza can learn a lesson."

He was talking to Luke. Luke was supposed to lift up this woman in his arms and take her to another place to be killed.

I have a choice. . . . I can make up my own mind. . . . The woman's words still seemed to be echoing in the room, reverberating in Luke's mind. *Do* I *have a choice?* he wondered. If he refused Officer Houk's order, he didn't think Officer Houk would smile and put his gun away and say, *Oh, you're right. We'll just leave this old lady alone. Have a nice day, ma'am.* Officer Houk would probably decide to shoot the woman *and* Luke.

But if he obeyed . . . if he played a role in her death . . .

Oh, Trey, why didn't you think about something like this happening, back when you said we should sabotage the Population Police from within? Luke agonized.

"Pick her up now!" Officer Houk shouted. "Do it!"

Luke stumbled forward and scooped the woman into his arms. Her body was incredibly light, like chicken bones. He thought about running out the back door to carry her to safety, but Officer Houk had the gun pointed at both of them now. Luke couldn't ever run fast enough or far enough.

Luke lowered his head, putting his face against the woman's cloud of white hair.

"I'm sorry," he whispered. "I'll try—"

The woman gave no sign that she'd heard him.

Officer Houk guided them out the doorway. Luke tripped over the broken sidewalk, and barely managed to keep from dropping the woman.

"Watch it!" Office Houk hissed.

"It's because of my leg," Luke tried to explain. "When the door hit—" His leg was throbbing now, and even the woman's slight weight seemed too much of a burden.

"Put her down here, then," Officer Houk said, pointing to a spot on the ground in front of a gathering crowd.

It seemed wrong to just drop such an old woman into the mud. But she surprised him by sliding down and standing on her own two feet. The crowd took in the sight of the regal old lady being held at gunpoint and fell silent.

"This woman," Officer Houk shouted at the crowd,

"refused to obey a direct order from a Population Police officer. This is treason. This is punishable by death. I hereby proclaim her sentence. Do all of you understand her crime?"

The crowd stayed silent. Luke saw tears rolling down the face of a girl in the front row. He saw a man holding his hand over his mouth, in horror.

And he heard from behind him a muffled "Sir?"

It was the driver, back in the jeep. "Sir," he hissed. "The radio—I think you should listen . . ."

Officer Houk frowned, obviously annoyed by the interruption. He glanced back and forth between the jeep and the crowd, between the straight-backed, silent woman and the radio the driver was holding out to him.

"Here," Officer Houk said, thrusting the gun into Luke's hand. "Keep pointing it at her," he whispered.

The metal of the gun handle seemed to burn against Luke's skin. *I have a choice. . . . I have a choice. . . .* The words seemed to roar in Luke's ears, blocking out almost every sound. Dimly, Luke was aware of Officer Houk walking back toward the jeep, muttering into the radio. Was the crowd murmuring now, too? What was Officer Houk hearing over the crackle of static?

". . . resistance in Ryana . . . facing hostilities in several towns . . . calling all units back for reinforcement . . ."

Had Luke really heard that?

Officer Houk was lowering the radio from his ear, turning to face Luke and the woman again.

"Shoot her," he said. "Shoot her and let's go."

The gun shook in Luke's hand. He remembered one other time he'd held a gun in his hand, held all the power. *I have a choice. . . . I have a choice. . . .*

"Shoot her now!" Officer Houk screamed.

Refused to obey a direct order . . . This is treason . . . punishable by death . . .

Luke dropped the gun and ran.

CHAPTER FIVE

Luke crashed through overgrown shrubs, dodged behind falling-down shacks. He heard gunshots behind him, but he didn't stop to see who was shooting whom, or whether anyone was shooting at him. He ran faster than he'd ever run in any game of football or kick-ball or spud; he ran without stopping even when his leg ached and his breath came in ragged gasps.

And then he fell to the ground and couldn't get back up. He lay in a heap for uncountable minutes, and then he rolled over on his back to stare straight up at the sky. Wispy clouds covered a dim, faraway sun, and then all of it blurred into a sea of gray.

He was crying. That was why everything looked so blurry.

Luke wiped his sleeve across his face, smearing clumps of dirt onto his skin. Dizzily, he raised himself up on his arms.

I didn't shoot her, he thought. *Oh, thank God, I didn't shoot her.*

The tears kept coming, and it didn't matter, because no one could see him. He was out in an empty field alone, and as far as he could tell, no one had followed him.

I should hide, he thought, but he didn't move. He sat there with broken cornstalks and clods of dirt poking at him, his muscles throbbing and his lungs still desperate for air. And somehow it was almost as comforting as leaning against his horse Jenny, letting her slide her warm nose under his arm.

I'm free, he thought. *I made my choice.*

His legs began to feel pleasantly numb, and his breathing slowed to a normal rate. Then a frightening thought crawled into his mind: *I could freeze.*

Ice crystals glistened in the mud around him, and now there was a frosty haze in the air. The weather was changing. Carefully Luke rose to his feet, the numbness giving way to pins and needles and pain. He stood, swaying unsteadily, and looked around. The field was surrounded by trees on all sides, but one direction led back to the village, one direction led out to the road, and one direction seemed to lead to yet another field. Painstakingly Luke began walking away from all that, toward the only place where the trees were thickly clumped.

Like the woods back home, Luke thought, and he had to choke back another sob that threatened to come bursting out. For most of his life, Luke's family had owned a huge woods beyond the edge of their backyard. Luke had never been allowed to go into the woods, but they had been his shield from the outside world, the protection that allowed him to play and work outside rather than cower in the house all day. Only when the Government forced Luke's family to sell the woods did Luke realize how trapped he was. Only then did he begin to long for freedom.

And only Jen told me freedom was possible, Luke thought with a pang.

He reached the edge of the woods and fought his way in through brambles and thorns. He had some vague notion of constructing a shelter for himself, just a place to stay until he could figure out what to do next. Just a place to stay until he stopped seeing the old woman staring at him every time he closed his eyes, until every random thought stopped throwing him into anguish. But most of the trees around him were soaring and thick-trunked, much too large to be felled by anything smaller than an ax or a chainsaw. The smaller trees and underbrush were worthless, barely fit to shelter a mouse or a squirrel.

Then the trees ended, and a wall of rock rose up before him. In spite of himself, Luke stared in amazement. He was used to flat farmland or, at most, gently rolling hills. This made him think of the mountains he'd seen only in books, the kind of thing he'd had to pretend to know about when he was attending school under a fake identity.

It's a wonder everyone didn't see through me, didn't know how ignorant I was, Luke thought. *I never knew mountains were like this.*

In awe, he ran his hands along the rock, his fingers tracing the crevices. He found layers of different colored rock, some that chipped away easily and some that held firm even when he pried against them with a stick. One of the layers led down at an angle; following it, Luke found an opening in the rock that seemed to lead deep into the mountain.

A cave, Luke thought, struggling to remember definitions and explanations he'd memorized for tests, never expecting the knowledge to have any use in the real world. *Caves have a constant temperature, summer and winter. People used to live in caves.*

Luke had found his shelter.

He crawled in, keeping his head down because the ceiling of the cave was only four or five feet above the ground. But it was warmer the farther he got from the opening. He slid back as far as he could go and still see, and he curled up against a wall of rock. He felt safer than he'd felt at any time since he'd joined the Population Police, maybe any time since the Government had torn down the woods behind his family's house.

He was just beginning to drift off to sleep when he heard the gunfire start up again.

CHAPTER SIX

The gunshots didn't sound nearby, but there were so many of them. When he'd been running away from Chiutza, he'd heard a *pop! pop! pop!* . . . Three or four shots. That had been frightening enough, and maybe in his fear and desperation he'd miscounted or misheard.

This gunfire was even more terrifying, because it sounded like dozens of guns all firing at once, and firing again and again and again.

War, Luke thought, straining again to remember a concept he'd studied in school and never expected to encounter for real. *Lots of people fighting.*

Luke's first instinct was to curl up more tightly in the safety of his cave, his knees against his chin, his body protected by thick rock from any and every bullet. He was willing to slide on into sleep, just so he wouldn't have to hear the sounds of anyone else's struggle.

But then, unbidden, another memory forced its way into his mind: Jen arguing with him the day before she died.

You can be a coward and hope someone else changes the world for you. You can hide up in that attic of yours until someone knocks at your door and says, "Oh, yeah, they freed the hidden. Want to come out?" Is that what you want?

She'd been trying to get him to come to the rally with her, the one protesting for third children's rights. She'd yelled at him that if he didn't play a role in seeking his own freedom, he'd always regret it: *When you don't have to hide anymore, even years from now, there'll always be some small part of you whispering, "I don't deserve this. I didn't fight for it. I'm not worth it." And you are, Luke, you are. . . .*

Substitute the word "cave" for "attic" and she might as well be arguing with him now. He shivered with the same kind of chills he would have felt if Jen's ghost had appeared to him and urged, *Get out of this cave this instant! Go and fight in that war!*

"Stop," he muttered, pressing his hands over his ears, as if that could shut out a voice he heard only in his own mind. "Why should I listen to you? It's not like your rally did any good. It only got you killed. Do you want me to die too?"

But he couldn't really argue that Jen's rally had been useless. So much had happened since then. Luke himself would never have gotten his fake I.D. and left home if it hadn't been for Jen and her rally. He never would have gone to Hendricks School or met any of his friends there. He never would have helped a boy named Smits come to terms with his brother's death. He never would have infiltrated

Population Police headquarters, never tried to make a difference in the world, never ended up here in this cave.

And that's supposed to convince me? he wondered.

Still, he took his hands off his ears and crawled back toward the cave's opening. Peeking out, he could see nothing but trees, a peaceful scene. But the sounds of gunfire were even louder. Maybe the battle wasn't so far away, after all.

I don't know who's fighting whom. I wouldn't know which side to join. I don't have a weapon—I'd be killed for sure.

He was still arguing with Jen, and she'd been dead for nearly a year.

Sighing, Luke slipped out of his cave and stood upright. He could just go see what was going on. He'd hide and watch. Surely it wouldn't be dangerous if he didn't get too close.

He began walking toward the sounds of battle, but the noise echoed in the trees, confusing him. Twice he got turned around and found himself walking back toward the mountainside. Or maybe it was the mountain that curved around, hugging the woods on more than one side.

He'd just started to feel confident that he was walking in the right direction when suddenly the shooting stopped. He froze, waiting, but the woods were silent again. And then he heard whoops and hollers off in the distance—off in the distance, but getting closer.

Luke slid behind a tree and crouched down, trusting that the shadows would hide him.

"Woo-hoo! We showed them, didn't we?"

"Did you see their faces right before they turned tail and ran?"

The voices were barely close enough for Luke to make out the words. But he could hear the laughter, the trampling feet.

One other time Luke had stood behind a tree in a shadowy wood, eavesdropping. That time he'd been brave enough to jump out and announce his presence, to lay down a challenge. But he'd witnessed a lot of awful things since then; he'd been betrayed as well as encouraged, tortured as well as rescued from torture.

This time he stayed behind his tree.

Eventually the voices and the laughter and the footsteps faded into the distance again. Luke waited in the shadows a while longer, wondering, *What was that all about? Which side were those people on? Were they involved in the shootings? Who were they fighting against? Who ran away?*

Luke remembered his own desperate fleeing, and the same sick panic flowed over him once again. He tamped it down, trying to think logically. The voices couldn't have been talking about him. He was just one person, not a "them."

But I was with other people—Officer Houk and the driver and the other boy. Luke had not let himself wonder what they'd done after he dropped the gun and ran. In his mind, the scene in the village of Chiutza had frozen the minute he left, like in some magical fairy tale. It was almost as if he believed he could wander back into the village now and still find the gun on the ground, the old lady standing straight and tall and defiant, the crowd with their mouths open in little circles of horror and disbelief, Officer Houk leaning against the jeep, holding the radio, his eyes popping out of his head. But of course that was wrong—something had happened after Luke ran away. Somebody had fired a gun, and a lot of somebodies had been firing a lot of guns since then. Luke couldn't go back and cower in his cave again without finding out who and what and how and why.

Grimacing, Luke stood up and began inching forward again. After a few paces, he could hear the voices again—not actual words, exactly, but he could catch the tone of triumph and glee. He turned and followed the voices at a distance, trying to tread as silently as possible. He didn't think that occasional snapping twigs or rustling leaves would alert anyone, but each sound was enough to send him back into a panic anyway. It was all he could do to force himself to keep going.

Jen, you were lucky, he thought, wanting to argue with a ghost again. *You planned your actions; you were in charge; you didn't have to deal with any mysteries.*

But of course that wasn't true, because Jen hadn't known what would happen at her rally. She hadn't been able to control the other third children who were supposed to go to the rally with her. She'd had no second sight, no special knowledge to protect her. She'd had only her own courage, and her own hope, and her own faith that freedom, when it came, would be worth the risk.

Luke reached the edge of the woods and was surprised to find himself on the outskirts of Chiutza. He hung back in the shadowy trees, listening to slamming doors and then silence. Everyone must have gone inside. All the houses were shut up against the cold—he could see smoke rising from chimneys and occasional shapes passing before windows, but no sound escaped.

Maybe if he waited until dark he could creep right up against one of the houses, press his ear against a wall and hear *something*. But after darkness fell he probably wouldn't be able to find his way back to his cave. He'd have no shelter, no protection against the long icy night.

Luke was still trying to decide what to do, when he saw a figure creep out of a shed behind one of the bigger houses. The figure was wearing a cloak, and it seemed to turn its head to peer directly at Luke out of the depths of the cloak's hood. Luke jerked behind the nearest tree, his heart pounding and the panic coursing through his body yet again. But when he dared to peek out a moment later, the figure was gone.

I'm safe, after all. He didn't see me. False alarm, Luke thought in relief.

And then a hand clamped over his mouth, and an arm clutched across his chest. Luke struggled to free himself, to scream, "Stop!" But a voice hissed in his ear, "Don't! Don't make a sound. Do you want to get us both killed?"

CHAPTER SEVEN

The hood of the cloak fell back and for the first time Luke could see the face of the person who'd attacked him.

It was the boy who'd ridden out to Chiutza in the jeep with him, the one who'd stolen Luke's cornbread and told him he stank.

"What—" Luke tried to ask, but the boy still had his hand covering Luke's mouth, his fingers holding Luke's jaw shut.

"This is my territory now," the boy said, still whispering into Luke's ear. "There's not room here for both of us. You go find some other place."

He shoved Luke away, and Luke sprawled in the dead leaves. He rolled over and looked up at the other boy.

"What are you talking about?" Luke asked. "What do you mean, 'territory'?"

Luke couldn't understand why the boy had attacked him and then shoved him away. He couldn't understand why the boy wasn't grabbing at him and shouting, *I found him! Here's the deserter! Officer Houk—over here!* Instead, the boy had said, "Do you want to get us both killed?" as if he were in as much trouble as Luke. Why?

"Shh," the boy said, glancing around nervously.

Understanding began to creep over Luke.

"Did you desert too?" Luke whispered.

The color drained from the boy's face.

"Don't say that," the boy hissed. "At least not if anyone from the Population Police comes back. *They* left *me* behind." A crafty look slid over his face. "Of course, if someone from Chiutza asks, maybe I did desert. Just not in front of everyone like you did."

Luke scrambled back up to his feet. He was secretly pleased when the other boy took a step back, like he was afraid of Luke. Luke was taller than the other boy, and Luke had muscles from his months of shoveling horse manure.

"So they left you behind," Luke repeated, trying to put it all together. He couldn't remember seeing the boy after those first few moments in Chiutza. Where had he been when Luke carried the old woman out of her house? Or when Officer Houk handed the gun to Luke?

"Well, yeah," the boy said. "After the villagers killed Officer Houk, do you think the driver waited around to make sure *I* was all right?"

Luke shook his head, not quite believing what he'd heard.

"What?" Luke said. "You mean, Officer Houk was—"

He broke off as someone opened a door in one of the Chiutzan houses. A girl stepped into the street and poured out a bowl of some sort of liquid. Both Luke and the other boy ducked down and held their breath until the girl went back into the house and shut the door.

"See? You almost gave us away. You have to leave," the boy said.

But this time Luke heard the fake bravado in the boy's voice, the fear and uncertainty trembling just below the surface.

"No," Luke said. "You have to tell me everything you saw."

"Not here," the boy said. "Someone will see us or hear us. And it's too cold."

Luke looked around, frowning, still trying to make sense of the boy's words. *After the villagers killed Officer Houk . . .* Luke saw the boy was beginning to inch away.

"We can talk in that shed over there," Luke said. "We'll whisper."

"The shed's mine!" the boy said, his voice arcing toward hysteria. "You can't have it! It's mine!"

Luke reached out and grabbed the boy's arm, to steady him and stop him from running away. Luke *had* to know what had happened.

"I don't want to take your shed away," Luke said, trying to make his voice soothing. "I've got my own place to stay. I just want to know what's going on."

"Where's your place?" the boy asked.

"Back there. In the woods," Luke said impatiently.

"Is it warm and dry? Do you have your own food supply?" the boy continued.

"I—" Luke began. His stomach churned, as if on cue. He hadn't thought about food at all since running away from Chiutza. He'd just thought about running and hiding and freedom and Jen. This made him wonder how clearly he'd been thinking all along, how sane any of his plans and actions had been. "Look," he said now, trying to sound calm and reasonable. Trying to *be* calm and reasonable. "I just want you to tell me what happened in Chiutza after I left. Then I'll leave you alone. I promise."

The other boy was staring at him warily, but when Luke gave a little tug on the boy's arm, he began to move toward the shed.

Twilight had fallen now, with long shadows extending from the woods into the village. It was no challenge for Luke and the other boy to creep along the edge of the woods, confident they were out of any villager's sight. But at the doorway to the shed Luke hesitated, sudden panic overtaking him.

What if this is all a trick? What if the boy was just pretending not to want me in the shed? What if Officer Houk and the driver are waiting there, with the gun? What if they plan to kill me on the spot for running away?

The other boy stepped across the threshold, into darkness.

"Coming?" he whispered, his voice taunting.

This shed's barely bigger than an outhouse, Luke told himself, fighting back the panic. *If Officer Houk and the driver were hiding in there, they'd have me by now, no matter what.*

Luke stepped in behind the boy and pulled the door shut behind them. Now the shed was completely dark, except for a patch of light on the opposite wall, where a board was broken away.

"This way," the boy muttered. "In case someone comes."

He pulled Luke over behind a pile of burlap grain sacks. The burlap smelled old and moldy, but Luke's stomach still grumbled at the thought of possible food within.

"We have to make a deal," the boy said.

"Huh?" Luke asked, distracted by the grain sacks and the trouble he was having getting his eyes to focus in the dark.

"A deal," the boy repeated. "I have something you want—information. What are you going to give me for it?"

Luke had nothing with him but the clothes on his back. And even those weren't his—they were the standard-issue shirt, pants, and boots that belonged to the Population Police.

"What do you want?" Luke asked, stalling for time.

"Oh, a gourmet meal would be great," the boy said. "That gun you were stupid enough to drop. Maybe a nice comfy bed so I don't have to sleep on burlap tonight?"

Somehow the boy's sarcasm seemed nastier in the dark.

I don't have anything to give you, Luke wanted to say. *What would it cost you just to tell me what I want to know for free?* But then he remembered the way the boy had grabbed the packet of cornbread before Luke had a chance to touch it, the way the boy had sneered about Luke smelling like horse manure.

"If you tell me what you saw after I ran out of Chiutza," Luke began, "I won't go knock on the door of that house over there. I won't tell them, 'Did you know there's a boy hiding in your shed, eating all your grain?'"

Luke wished so badly that he could see the boy's face, see how he was taking this threat.

"You wouldn't do that," the boy said finally, though his voice sounded thin and worried. "You'd be caught too."

"How do you know I wouldn't do that?" Luke asked. "The villagers saw me refuse to shoot one of their friends. Maybe I think they'd treat me like a hero. Maybe I'm already counting on them feeding me that gourmet meal to celebrate. Maybe I've been on their side all along."

"If you were, you'd know these people don't have any gourmet food," the other boy sputtered. "They're lucky to have grain, and that's probably not going to last the winter."

"Especially not with you eating it," Luke said, and somehow that came out sounding like the last word.

The boy cleared his throat, nervously. And then he began to talk.

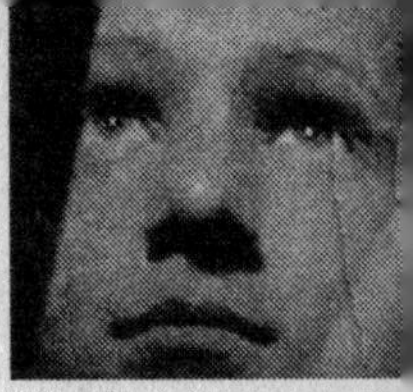

CHAPTER EIGHT

"I was doing what Officer Houk told me to do," the boy started defensively. "I knocked on every door I came to. I was just circling around to find out what street I was supposed to go to next, when I saw Officer Houk standing there in front of this big crowd, pointing a gun at a woman. I heard him say something about treason, and then I saw him hand the gun to you and tell you to shoot her. And then you dropped the gun and ran. Why didn't you do what you were told? Why didn't you obey?"

Now Luke wished he hadn't used such a heavy-handed bargaining technique. Why hadn't he just agreed to trade stories with the boy?

But that was a dangerous thought. Telling anything was risky.

"I—I didn't think the woman deserved to die," Luke said, choosing his words carefully.

"So?" the boy said. "Lots of people die who don't deserve it."

Luke frowned, trying to think how he could explain.

"I didn't want to be the one to shoot her," he said finally.

Luke thought maybe he could see the other boy shrugging in the darkness.

"What did she do, anyway?" the boy asked.

"She refused to come out to the meeting about the I.D.'s," Luke said. "She said that after everything else that had happened, she didn't care about identity cards." Luke couldn't quite see the other boy's face, but he could feel the boy looking incredulously at him. Luke felt like his words hadn't done the woman justice, hadn't conveyed the dignity in her defiance. "She was very brave," he added.

"That's brave?" the boy said. "Sounds stupid to me."

"You didn't see her," Luke said weakly.

"I saw her being held at gunpoint, condemned to death," the boy said. "If that's where bravery gets you, no thanks."

Luke swallowed hard. He felt like he and the other boy were engaged in some sort of competition, and the other boy had just scored the first point.

"But, after that," Luke said, "who shot Officer Houk?"

"I couldn't see exactly," the boy said. "A bunch of people rushed forward after you dropped the gun. Someone grabbed the gun and I could see it pointing at Officer Houk. Then there were a bunch of shots and Officer Houk fell over and stopped moving and the driver drove away . . . and I hid. I don't think anybody remembered about me. Nobody came looking for me."

The boy sounded almost forlorn at having been forgotten.

"And you've just been hiding out ever since?" Luke asked.

"Yeah. So?"

Luke remembered he hadn't exactly done anything dramatic and decisive himself.

"Are you going to try to get back to Population Police headquarters?" he asked.

"What's it to you? You scared I'll turn you in? Scared I'll say you disobeyed? Scared I'll say it was all your fault Officer Houk died?"

"No," Luke said, and it dawned on him that that was the truth. Somehow he wasn't afraid of that possibility. Population Police headquarters seemed very remote and far away now. "You don't even know my name."

"They kept records of who went with Officer Houk," the boy said. "They'll know I wasn't the one who disobeyed. Maybe they'd give me a reward for turning you in." He sounded hopeful now.

Luke remembered seeing a man writing names down on a clipboard as everyone else ran past him toward the jeeps. It hadn't been Luke's real name anyhow; he was on his second fake identity since leaving home.

"Nobody has any identity cards anymore, remember?" Luke said. "I could be anyone. It doesn't matter if you turn me in or not."

The boy sagged back against one of the burlap bags, and Luke thought, *I won this round.*

"It doesn't matter anyhow," the boy said, his bravado gone. "I heard people saying they've got all the roads blocked off around this area. I couldn't go back to Population Police headquarters if I wanted to. Did you hear the fighting?"

Luke nodded.

"Were they fighting the Population Police?" he asked.

"I reckon so," the boy said. "A bunch of men and boys came back into the village bragging about how the Population Police were cowards underneath their fancy uniforms, how they just dropped their weapons and ran. Like you did."

Luke thought there was a difference, but he wasn't going to argue about it with this boy.

"I think half the village is in that house over there, celebrating," the boy continued, pointing to the side. "I heard people shouting about how they don't have to listen to anybody else anymore—that they're in charge of their own lives now."

Free, Luke thought. *Is that what free is? Is everybody free now?*

"That's where I was going when I saw you. I was going to sneak over there and see if I could take some of the food they have at their party."

"What if someone saw you?" Luke asked.

"I'm not stupid like you, still wandering around in a Population Police uniform," the boy sneered. Luke felt his face go red. He hadn't thought to worry about his clothes.

He'd just been glad the uniform fabric was thick enough to protect him from the cold.

"I tore the Population Police insignia off my shirt, see?" the boy said, holding out a piece of material as proof. Luke brushed his hand against dangling threads. "And then I found this cloak on a clothesline, to cover it all up. I'm safe."

"What if the people are wrong, and the Population Police are still in control?" Luke challenged him.

"Well, then I can put the insignia right back on my shirt," the boy said. "I'm not going to throw it away. I could find a needle and thread, if I had to."

Luke frowned, not quite able to figure out why the boy's explanation bothered him so much. Was he just jealous that he hadn't thought to do that himself? Then he knew what he wanted to ask.

"But—are you glad if the Population Police are really gone? Or do you want them to stay in power? Which side are you really on?"

The boy laughed, as if Luke's question were the height of stupidity.

"Which side am I on?" he repeated. "What do you think? Whatever side feeds me—that's the one for me."

CHAPTER NINE

Luke kept his promise and stood up to leave the shed as soon as he'd heard the end of the boy's story.

"Well, uh, good luck," he said awkwardly. "Keep warm."

He waited for a second, half hoping the boy would say, *Hey, why don't we stick together? Be a team?* But Luke and the other boy hadn't trusted each other enough even to tell their names; Luke had no doubt that the boy would turn him in to the Population Police if he ever had a chance. So why did Luke's heart ache? Why did he suddenly feel so lonely as he moved toward the door?

I like being on a team, Luke thought. Even at Population Police headquarters, where he never saw anyone but Nina, he'd known he wasn't completely alone.

He was now.

Luke peeked out into the twilight gloom, then eased out the door and pulled it shut behind him. The merriment in the party house had gotten so raucous that he could hear shouts and bursts of song even through the thick walls.

Should I go try to join them? Luke wondered. *Nobody wanted to get rid of the Population Police more than I did.*

But Luke couldn't quite picture himself striding over to the house, thrusting open the front door, announcing himself to all those strangers who might or might not be on his side.

What if they've got no more loyalty than the boy in the shed?

Luke could imagine the room falling into a horrified silence, someone rushing over to beat him up. To kill him. He was still wearing a Population Police uniform, after all.

Luke stepped into the shadow of the woods and, despite the cold, took his shirt off. He shoved his arms through the sleeves backward, turning them inside out, and pulled the front panels of the shirt together that way. It was hard buttoning the shirt back up from the inside, especially with his fingers going numb in the cold. But he felt better with the hated Population Police insignia hidden.

Luke heard a door opening behind him, so he crouched down in the weeds and looked around. It was only the boy creeping out of the shed toward the party house. Luke watched, wondering how the boy intended to get any food from a closed-up house filled with people. The boy sidled up to a window that was missing several panes of glass. Some of the panes had been replaced by plastic and some by squares of cardboard. The boy pushed at one of the cardboard squares, squeezing his fingers under the bottom.

Even from a distance, Luke could see the triumphant smile on the boy's face. Luke imagined that the boy must have reached his hand into a bowlful of some great delicacy—raisins, maybe, or almonds. And then the boy's expression changed.

"Ow!" he howled.

He seemed to be trying to jerk his hand back, but his hand was caught somehow. The front door of the house opened and a horde of men rushed out, screaming, "Thief! Thief!" They circled the building, pulled the boy away from the window and threw him to the ground. Now the shouts were jumbled: One man growled, "There's Mary's cloak that was stolen," and everyone else seemed to be shouting, "Population Police! We'll show the Population Police who's in charge!"

"No, wait!" the boy shrieked. "I'm on your side! I'm the kid who risked his life refusing to shoot the old woman! It's because of me you got the gun—"

"We'll show you the gun!" someone shouted, and then everyone stepped back as one of the men pulled a gun out of his pocket and held it up in the air, where it glinted in the last rays of sunlight.

The man pointed the gun straight at the boy, making everyone else laugh. He stepped forward, pretending to be about to shoot, then lowered the gun at the last minute. He did this two or three times, and the men around him laughed all the harder as the boy squirmed on the ground in terror.

"Enough games," the man said, raising the gun yet again. "And enough of the Population Police, I say."

This time he cocked the gun and aimed carefully.

This is real, Luke thought. *This is really going to happen.*

"No, don't!" he screamed.

The man with the gun looked up, startled. His eyes searched the darkened woods. And then he aimed the gun at the tree where Luke was hiding and began shooting.

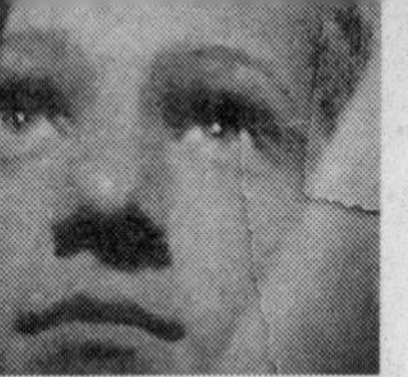

CHAPTER TEN

Luke ran.

Later he wouldn't remember much about the ground he covered, the logs he leaped over, the underbrush he trampled. His mind had no time to record such useless details. He ran with terror urging him on, a voice constantly in his head: *They're right behind you. They've got to be. They're about to catch up. They're going to shoot again and this time they won't miss. There! Did you hear that? What was that? They're about to grab you—*

He didn't turn around and look back. Even a second's lack of focus could have slammed him into a tree, snagged his feet on a root. He was so convinced he was about to be captured that he didn't worry about where he was running *to*—he just knew he had to get away.

So the sight of the mountain surprised him: The huge rock wall loomed directly in front of him. Automatically he veered to the right, then hesitated. *Was that—?* He saw telltale cracks in the rock, leading down to an opening at the mountain's base. He finally dared to slow down and glance over his shoulder—no one was directly behind him. He dived down and slid on his stomach across the rock floor.

Yes. It was a cave.

Luke had no way of knowing if it was the same cave he'd found before. He scuttled back into the darkness and huddled against a rock wall, his entire body shaking, his desperate gasps for breath echoing as loudly as a steam train. He finally captured enough air in his lungs that he could hold his breath for a few seconds and listen. Were those footsteps outside? Was someone even now about to duck down and crawl in after him? *I'd be trapped. There's no escape . . .* Luke stared at the thin sliver of gray light coming in through the cave's opening. No figure moved in to block the light. Maybe Luke hadn't heard footsteps. Maybe he'd been tricked by the sound of his own pulse beating in his ears.

His body had more tricks in store for him. His mind kept replaying the scene that he'd witnessed, slowing down for the final frame: the man turning, pointing the gun at Luke. Shooting. Luke tried not to let himself focus on the man and the gun. He kept trying to make himself remember what he'd seen out of the corner of his eye, right before fleeing. There, on the ground. Had the boy been crawling away? Had he slipped out between the men's legs while they weren't looking? Had he been able to escape?

Oh, please . . .

Luke couldn't even have said why the boy's life mattered so much to him. The boy had been no friend to Luke. He'd shared information only because he was scared. He'd refused to share shelter or food. Why had Luke risked his own life trying to save the other boy?

Isn't it enough that the boy was alive? Isn't that reason enough for me to want him to stay alive?

Luke remembered the boy's own comment on life and death: "Lots of people die who don't deserve it." If the roles had been reversed—if it had been Luke on the ground and the boy hiding in the woods—Luke didn't think the boy would have tried to save him.

I don't think like he does. I'm not that . . . free. But was it freedom not to care about anyone but yourself? Not to care what side you were on, as long as you got food in your stomach?

Luke's own stomach felt squeezed in and petrified, almost beyond hunger. But he knew he wouldn't survive long without nourishment. *Tomorrow. Tomorrow I'll have to find food.* For now, even if his life depended on it, he couldn't force himself to crawl back out of his cave.

CHAPTER ELEVEN

For a long time, Luke lay huddled against the rock wall, his ears straining to interpret every sound. Was that rustling noise a squirrel running through the fallen leaves or a person approaching Luke's cave? Was that scratching noise the wind blowing a twig against the mountain or a human lighting a match?

Eventually Luke slipped into a fitful sleep haunted by nightmares of guns firing and people chasing him. The woman he'd refused to shoot appeared in his dreams, but she never said anything. She just kept looking at Luke—why was she looking at him? The boy Luke had tried to save sat at a table spread with every delicious food Luke had ever seen, but every time Luke tried to approach, the boy said, "Oh, no, this is *my* gourmet meal. Nobody can make me share." The stiff threads of the Population Police insignia stabbed against his chest, and he tore at it in his sleep, not sure if the pain was imaginary or real.

When Luke woke up the next morning, he felt weak and

trembly. His head ached from sleeping on rock, and his legs and arms felt bruised. He lay staring at the faint light filtering in through the cave's opening. He blinked one eye and then the other, making the light shift position, jump from side to side. That was the kind of thing he used to entertain himself with more than a year ago, when he was bored and lonely, hiding in his parents' attic. Before he met Jen.

You didn't shoot the woman. You tried to save the boy. Stop hiding, Luke. You're worth it, you really are. . . .

Luke decided this cave had to be the same one he'd discovered the day before, because it, too, was haunted by Jen's voice.

Get up. Go. Get out of here. Stop hiding.

"All right, all right," Luke muttered.

He stretched and started to stand up, forgetting how low the cave's ceiling was. His head slammed against solid rock.

"Ow! Oooh—thanks a lot, Jen. Got any other great advice?"

He rubbed his throbbing head and half crawled, half slithered toward the cave's entrance. Then he sat there, peering out into the waiting woods. He needed food—to be able to think clearly, if nothing else. Maybe with food he'd even stop thinking that he could talk to ghosts. Chiutza had to be the nearest place with food, but every time he started thinking about heading in that direction, his legs shook and his heart felt like it was quivering in his chest.

I don't have to go there, he told himself. *Maybe I'll just go . . . back.*

He wasn't quite sure what he meant by "back." He had such a jumble of images in his head. He could see himself showing up at home, his mother's arms wrapped around him, her face glowing with joy at the sight of him. He could see himself returning to the school he'd attended, his old headmaster, Mr. Hendricks, rolling out in his wheelchair, crying, "Oh, Luke, it's so good to see that you're safe." He could see himself back at the stables, with his favorite horse, Jenny, whinnying and rubbing her nose contentedly against his arm. Luke thought that all of those places—home, Hendricks School, Population Police headquarters—were to the east. The sun had been behind him the whole time he'd been traveling yesterday morning. If he just walked toward the sun now, surely he'd eventually get someplace he wanted to go. It made sense, didn't it?

Luke stepped out of his cave and began walking.

His legs were wobbly and his throat was parched, but the cool air and the motion cleared his head a little. If the other boy had been right the night before, if the Population Police were really out of power, Luke had plenty of reason for rejoicing. When he got away from Chiutza, maybe he'd even find someone who'd help him get home. He'd be done with Population Police headquarters, done with boarding school—he could live a normal life with his own family.

And if the boy was wrong? If he was lying?

Luke thought he could handle that possibility too. The Population Police had been in power in one way or another his entire life. He'd survived. If the Population Police stopped him now, he could . . . he could use the other boy's story, just like the other boy had tried to use Luke's.

I was on a mission to hand out new identity cards in Chiutza. The villagers attacked the officer in charge, and then the driver sped away. I didn't desert. I was abandoned.

Luke didn't let himself think about how badly pretending had worked for the other boy. He didn't let himself wonder if the other boy had been killed after all.

Luke hadn't been walking for very long when he came to a stream gurgling with cool, clear water. He bent down to drink, taking long swallows from his cupped hands. As he rose, he saw that the stream led out of the woods toward a vast expanse of open land—another field. At the edge of the field was a row of trampled plants that Luke recognized as soybeans. For some reason, they'd escaped harvest. They'd been battered by the winter winds and snow and ice, but Luke could still see seed pods hanging from the thin, bent stems. Luke rushed over and pulled off pod after pod, cracking them open and tossing the withered beans into his mouth. It was hardly a gourmet meal, but Luke was so relieved to have something to chew, something to swallow. He was so absorbed in eating that it took him a few minutes to remember to look around, to be cautious.

That was when he saw the truck.

CHAPTER TWELVE

It was traveling down a road on the other side of the field, its engine purring, its tires rolling smoothly. Luke was pretty sure the truck's driver wouldn't have any reason to glance his way, but he crouched down anyway, flattening his body against the cold dirt.

The engine's hum changed, from speeding along to idling, Luke thought.

Did he see me? Is the driver climbing out of his truck to come and get me? Terror pinned Luke to the ground. He wanted to run, but he didn't seem to have control over his legs anymore.

Then he heard someone yell, "Hey, get that off the road! I'm on official Population Police business!"

Was the Population Police business coming to look for Luke? Did they know what he had done?

Gunfire sounded, and then the horn of the truck began to blare, endlessly, as if something or someone had fallen against it and wouldn't or couldn't move.

Then the blaring stopped, and another voice shouted out, "That's what we think of official Population Police business!"

Luke lay flat on the ground, his heart pounding, his mind scrambling to make sense of what he'd heard. Someone had blocked the road—the rebels? Someone had been shot—the person driving the Population Police truck?

There was a creaking sound, like metal doors being opened.

"Yee-haw! Look at all this food!" yet another voice screamed.

Luke couldn't quite make out the rest of the shouting because several voices were yelling at once—something like "It's all ours, now!" and maybe "I'd just like to see the Population Police try to take it back. Hear that, Poppies?"

Silently, Luke inched back toward the woods. Once he was under cover of the trees, he stood again and tiptoed as quickly as he could away from the direction of the road. His heart wouldn't stop pounding; he couldn't keep from turning his head from side to side compulsively, trying to look all around him all at once. He startled every time he heard a chipmunk running up a tree, a squirrel rustling in the leaves.

Why am I so scared? he wondered. *I wanted to see the Population Police overthrown. I dreamed about it. I was working toward that goal. If they're out of power, shouldn't I be happy?* He kept hearing the gunfire and the blaring horn echoing in his mind. He kept shivering with fear. *But they were attacking the Population Police. My enemies. Shouldn't the enemies of my enemies be my friends?*

He couldn't help wondering about the person driving that truck on official Population Police business, delivering food. Had it been someone who truly believed in the Population Police cause, who wanted to see third children dead? Or had it been someone like Luke, who'd joined up solely to sabotage the Population Police from inside—who'd maybe ended up dying for a cause he opposed? Maybe it had been someone like the boy back in Chiutza, who'd joined the Population Police just to get food, who would join any cause that fed him. Did that make it wrong for the rebels to have killed him?

Luke was confused. He was lost now too. He'd had no problem walking toward the east when the sun was low in the sky, but now it was almost directly overhead. He kept tilting his head back, looking up, and the sun seemed to waver, all depending on how he held his head.

"Just keep walking in the same direction, stupid," he muttered to himself. But that was easier said than done when he constantly had to dodge around trees, step over fallen logs, duck under low-hanging branches. He could never be sure that he was aiming in the right direction. What if he was walking straight back to Chiutza?

They saw me in a Population Police uniform before. They'd remember me. . . . They'd recognize my voice from last night. . . . The terror coursed through Luke's body so strongly, it was all he could do to keep walking. He couldn't let himself think about anything except placing one foot down and then the other.

Shortly after what Luke guessed to be noon, when the sun began to drop a little in the sky, the woods directly ahead of him thinned out. He slowed down his stride, became even more careful to avoid stepping on twigs or into piles of dry, rustly leaves. He could see roofs and walls—*was* it Chiutza again? Then he noticed how many of the walls were broken off and crumbling, how many of the roofs had gaping holes open to the sky. It wasn't Chiutza. Chiutza had been run-down and ramshackle but patched up. This village was in total ruins.

Luke crept forward, watching for any sign of humans: smoke from the chimneys, perhaps, or the sound of a baby crying, or the smell of cooking stew. But the tumbledown houses and huts before him were silent and still. Timidly Luke stepped into the clearing around the village. He held his breath, listening harder. All he could hear was the wind blowing through empty window frames, making the same kind of lonely howl it had made blowing through empty branches in the woods.

There were no people in this village. Luke was so sure of it that he walked to the exact center of the houses and huts—what had once been the village square, perhaps. A rutted dirt road led out of the village, but it looked as if no one had driven down it in a long, long time.

"Where did everyone go?" he muttered, truly puzzled.

He knew about the droughts and famines years ago, before he was born. That was the reason the Government had instituted the Population Law, the one that made it illegal for people to have more than two children. According to the Government, there had been too many people.

This village looked like there hadn't been enough people—not enough to fill the houses, to patch the roofs, to putty the walls, to trim back the trees.

Luke pushed against the door of one of the houses. It creaked back on rusty hinges, revealing a room full of broken chairs and tattered wallpaper.

Did the people leave quickly? Luke wondered. *Or did they have time to pack, to sort out what they wanted to take and what they wanted to leave behind?* His stomach growled, reminding him that this wasn't just a philosophical question. *Did they leave any food?*

He walked on through the house to a kitchen in the back, where linoleum peeled up from the floor, a sink dangled from a rotted board, and rusty pipes hung out from the wall. He left muddy footprints across the linoleum, but he didn't see how that could matter. He opened cupboard doors, hoping for canned food—canned food and maybe a can opener, too, for good measure. Or maybe jars of preserves like his mother used to prepare every year, with every fruit and vegetable that came into season. He remembered the rows of corncobs cooling on her kitchen counters, the bushel baskets full of tomatoes, the cooked apples she always let him smash up into sauce. His mouth watered and his eyesight blurred, making it hard to see that the cupboards in front of him now were bare.

Of course they're bare, Luke told himself. *Of course there's no food. People were starving, remember? They wouldn't have left any food behind.*

He slipped to the floor, bending his head down in despair against his knees. He was so hungry. He was so tired. He'd walked so far and been so scared for so long—what would it hurt if he rested for just a few minutes? He tilted sideways until he was lying on the floor, his head resting against a coil of the linoleum that had been heaved up from the decaying floor. He wrapped his arms around his knees, drawing them toward his chest.

Just for a few minutes, he told himself, slipping almost instantly off to sleep.

The next thing he knew there were voices talking. Talking in the same house he was in.

CHAPTER THIRTEEN

"But sir, this is an unauthorized village," someone was arguing from the front room of the house. "Can't you see no one's been here in years?"

"A lot has happened lately that the Population Police didn't authorize," another voice growled. "Our orders are to search every house in every village we come to and kill any unauthorized person we find. And we will follow orders."

Luke's eyes sprang open. With his head against the linoleum, he had a clear line of sight to the muddy footprints he'd tracked across the floor. He scrambled up, and began frantically scrubbing the mud away with his sleeve. But that just left streaks.

They'll still be able to see that it's fresh mud.

"The Population Police will prevail," the growly voice went on. "We always have. It's just a matter of time."

The sound of footsteps echoed through the house, moving closer to the kitchen.

Did I leave muddy footprints everywhere? Luke wondered. *How much time do I have before they notice?*

He was standing now, glancing around for any exit. Why hadn't he looked for anything in the kitchen besides food? Incredibly enough, the window in this room wasn't broken, and when Luke shoved against the window frame, it seemed to be warped permanently shut. But beneath the window there was a hole in the wall, a place where mold had eaten the drywall away and the boards behind didn't meet exactly. Luke thought it looked like small animals had crawled in and out through that hole—raccoons, perhaps, or possums. Could Luke fit through too?

He didn't have time to measure carefully. He dived for the hole, shoving his shoulders against the rotting, splintering wood. Even if the men in the house didn't notice the fresh mud on the floor, they'd certainly see this enlarged hole.

What other choice do I have?

Luke broke through and landed in a thicket outside. He rolled onto his feet and around glanced quickly—he saw just the bumper of some vehicle parked at the front of the house, but no sign of other Population Police officials wandering through the ruins. He took off running for the woods.

"Hey! You! Stop! We're the Population Police!" someone yelled behind him.

Luke tried to run faster, but it was hard with his legs so stiff and sore. He'd run so much the day before; he'd used up so much of his energy walking all morning.

"You can't escape! We'll find you! We'll hunt you down!"

Luke crashed into the woods, and it was like a flashback to his terror-stricken dreams the night before: running, being chased, nowhere to go, nowhere to hide . . .

"We're still in charge!" someone shouted behind him. How far away was the voice? Was it just behind him or several yards back, still in the ruins of the village?

Maybe Luke was a little delirious; maybe his brain wasn't getting enough oxygen to think straight. For whole minutes, he had trouble remembering whom he was running from: the Population Police officers doing their house-to-house search? The Chiutzan villager with the gun? Officer Houk? Somehow Luke's legs were carrying him so fast that his eyes couldn't absorb the sights around him quickly enough. Trees. Grass. Sky. Branches. No more branches. Lots more sky. Houses. Faces. A lot of faces, all looking down at him.

Luke blinked, fighting an awful blackness.

"I think he's passing out," someone said. A woman. The voice seemed to come from a million miles away. Luke knew he couldn't surrender to unconsciousness now. He forced his eyes back open, trying to focus on the circle of faces around him.

"Here. Here's something to drink," a new voice said, and someone poured liquid down his throat. Luke couldn't have said whether it was cold or hot, water or broth. But somehow it brought him back to himself. He struggled to sit up.

"Got—to—go—," he moaned, trying to get his muscles to work, to pull himself upright, to propel himself forward again.

"Easy there, pal." It was a man's voice this time. Friendly-sounding. Luke tried to focus on the source of the voice, the face of the man who had spoken. He saw white whiskers, blue eyes, a craggy nose. "I don't think you're going to be able to go anywhere for a while. Not on your own, anyway. Where were you trying to get to? Was someone chasing you?"

"Yes," Luke whispered.

"Who was it?"

Dizzily, Luke managed to stand, though he didn't quite trust his legs to hold him up. He rubbed his hand across his face. Which side would these people be on? Would they be like the villagers back in Chiutza—eager to attack the Population Police? Or would they be Population Police sympathizers—eager to help Luke if he said he worked for the Population Police, eager to turn him in if he didn't?

"Is that a Population Police uniform you're wearing?" someone asked.

Luke kept his hand over his eyes. Through the slits between his fingers, he tried to peer out at the faces around him, to gauge their expressions. Anxious? Angry? Sympathetic? Luke couldn't tell. Was it good or bad that he still had the shirt of his uniform turned inside out? Which side of the shirt would these people rather see? Luke had had to lie and pretend so much during the past year, ever since leaving home. What was he supposed to do now, when he had no way of knowing which lie would save him, which pretense would keep him alive?

Maybe he'd have to tell the truth.

"I—I'm running away from the Population Police," he said. "I deserted. They wanted me to shoot someone and I . . . I didn't want to do that."

He kept his body hunched over, cowering. He dreaded the moment when he'd have to look up and see how the people around him had reacted to his words. But nobody spoke for a long time. Luke heard a car engine approaching, then idling. He heard a familiar, growling voice shout out, "Population Police! Submit to a house-to-house search! Show all your identification papers! Turn in any unauthorized persons!"

He felt his body begin to quiver, his muscles turn to helpless jelly, his dread turn to paralyzing certainty.

Then he heard another voice, just as loud, coming from someone in the circle around him. This voice spoke only one word:

"No."

CHAPTER FOURTEEN

The man with the whiskers linked his arm with Luke's right elbow; a woman did the same thing on his other side. Together they lifted him upright. Around them others were joining arms, shifting positions. The circle was transforming itself into a straight line, strong and true. Strong and true and facing a Population Police officer in a fancy car.

"Go away," the man with the whiskers said. "You're not wanted here."

"But—I have a gun!" the officer sputtered.

"Yes," the man said calmly. "You have a gun. But there are just two of you, and there are many of us. You couldn't kill us all. Not when we are standing together. You have no control over us anymore."

Luke felt the power in the man's words like something physical—a presence as distinct as the man and woman standing on either side of him, holding him up. The Population Police officer seemed to feel it too. He shrank back a little in his seat. He didn't seem inclined to shout anymore about how the Population Police were still in charge.

"Hand over that boy, at least, and I'll leave you alone," he offered finally. "That boy is not one of yours. He's nothing to you, I'd wager."

Luke knew that the Population Police officer was talking about him. He was the only one with twigs in his hair, the only one panting, the only one wearing an inside-out Population Police shirt. How much did the officer know? That Luke had been in the abandoned village? That he'd been in Chiutza? Fear made Luke's legs weak; the whole world seemed to spin around him.

But the man and woman on either side of him kept a firm grip on his arms.

"He's one of ours now," the woman said.

The Population Police officer stared at Luke, at the woman, at the man. His gaze seemed to take in the whole line of people united against him. Then he leaned forward and tapped his driver's shoulder.

"We'll go now," he said.

The driver looked back, his face confused.

"You're letting them get away with this?" he asked. "You're not even going to shoot the boy?"

"I said go!" the officer roared.

The driver shrugged, then bent down and slipped the car into gear. It leaped forward, its engine noise loud and angry. As the car drove away, the noise faded into a faint buzz in the distance.

And then into nothingness. Silence. The Population Police were gone.

Luke stood shoulder to shoulder with a whole line of people—men and women, boys and girls—people he didn't even know who had just saved his life. Everyone stayed quiet, keeping their arms linked; it seemed like they, too, were having a hard time believing what had happened.

"Thank you," Luke mumbled. "Thank you." He swallowed hard. "But why—why did you help me?"

He looked up beseechingly at the man with the whiskers. The man was staring far off into the distance.

"It was the right thing to do," the man finally said. "We let them bully us into doing the wrong thing much too often in the past. It was time for a change."

The others in the line were nodding and murmuring in agreement. They dropped arms and broke off into little clumps, whispering and reliving the thrill of sending the Population Police away. Some of the younger children even began to giggle as they mimicked the official's panic.

These people were strangers, but they had become very precious to Luke. He worried that they were too innocent.

"What if the Population Police come back?" Luke asked. "They could bring hundreds of men, hundreds of guns. It isn't safe, what you did, showing that you disagree. You should leave now, while you have the chance, run away—"

"We won't run," the woman on Luke's other side said. "Look at us. Don't you see that we're going to die anyway?

If the Population Police come back, we will die a little sooner. But our consciences will be clear."

For the first time Luke noticed how thin all the people were. Their faces were gaunt, the hollows in their cheeks incredibly deep. The wrists and ankles that stuck out from their tattered clothes were little more than bone.

"You're starving," he whispered.

"We don't have enough food to survive the winter," the man said with a hopeless shrug. "We petitioned the Population Police for help, but they said it was our own fault, our own problem. We made a pact after that, that we would not listen to them anymore. We would not be . . . weak."

"You're giving up," Luke said in disbelief.

"We're free," the man replied.

CHAPTER FIFTEEN

As little food as they had, the people insisted on sharing it with Luke.

"This was our declaration of independence," the woman said. "We should have a celebration—a feast!"

The feast was hard bread served with broth that might have once had a passing acquaintance with a potato or two. But Luke sat in a warm room to eat it—these people had plenty of firewood. They clustered around him eagerly, telling him their names. The man who had done most of the talking was Eli; the woman was Adriana. Luke was also introduced to Jasper and Lett and Alice and Simon and Hadley and Sarah and Randall. He couldn't keep track of which identity went with which face, but he treasured the sound of the names piling up around him like so many golden coins. He hadn't known the name of anyone he'd met since he'd left for Chiutza.

"And you are . . . ?" Eli asked.

Luke hesitated. He had two fake names he could use. At

school he'd been Lee Grant; at Population Police headquarters he'd been Wendell Smathers. But each name came with baggage; each carried dangers of its own.

"Luke," he said. "I'm Luke."

As soon as he said it, he thought that he could easily have just made up a name—it wasn't as though these people were going to check for identity cards or papers.

But if the Population Police come back . . .

These people wouldn't turn him in. They'd already had their chance to do that.

They could have handed me over in exchange for food. Why didn't they think of that? What if they think of it now?

The room seemed too warm suddenly; the people were crowded in too closely, their bony elbows and shoulders and hips poking against him. *When I have nightmares tonight, I'm going to dream about skeletons,* Luke thought. The bread suddenly seemed too dry to chew and he began to choke.

Someone pounded him on the back.

"There, there," Eli said. "You might want to eat a little more slowly. Savor it, you know?"

He sounded so wistful that some of Luke's panic slipped away.

I don't think *they'd turn me in, even now,* he decided. *But I still have to stay alert.*

"How is it that you showed up in our village?" Eli asked. "Except for the Population Police, we haven't had an outsider here in ages."

Luke calculated what he could safely tell.

"I was running away from the Population Police. I wanted to go home. I fell asleep in an abandoned village over . . ." Luke wanted to point toward the ruins, but he'd gotten disoriented.

Eli nodded anyway.

"Over there," he said, pointing past the fireplace. "Yes. Go on."

"When I woke up, I heard voices—the Population Police. I . . . I panicked and ran away, and they heard me, and so I ran more. . . . It was just luck that I ended up here."

Eli kept nodding.

"Ah," he said. "Then you've seen our true homes."

"You mean that old village? The ruins?" Luke asked skeptically.

"They weren't ruins when we lived there," Eli said, shaking his head slowly, his white beard swaying. "We had beautiful houses, lush gardens. Then the droughts came. The Government said we had to move. They said we were too far off their main supply lines. We didn't fit in their plans. We were inconvenient."

"We thought they would save us from starving," Adriana said, "so of course we did what they said."

She poured more broth into Luke's bowl and watched him spoon it up to his mouth, as if she could get her nourishment from watching him eat.

Eli went on with his story. "Then they said we couldn't have gardens anymore, because it was an inefficient use of the land. They said we couldn't grow flowers, because that was a waste. They said we had to grow soybeans instead of corn one year, corn instead of soybeans the next. There were rules on top of rules. Anything we grew had to go right back to the Government. Then they would give us what we were allowed to eat—if we met our quota."

"We never grew enough," Adriana whispered.

Luke thought about the cold, hard soil he'd fallen down on. Then he thought about the rich, dark, loamy dirt of his family's farm.

"Maybe your soil isn't right for corn and soybeans," Luke offered.

"That's what we told the Government, but they never listened," Eli said. "They weren't people who knew about soil. They'd just point at numbers on their forms and yell at us, 'We have you down for this many bushels this year. Got it?'"

Luke remembered how he'd pictured the Government as some big, fat, bossy man when he'd been a little kid. That image seemed so innocent now.

"Then they took away everyone they could to work for the Population Police," Adriana said. "We haven't seen any of them since."

"James," Eli said. "Aileen. Twila. Sue. Peter. Robin. Jonathan. Detrick. Lester. Sal. . . ."

It took Luke a moment to realize that Eli was listing all the people the village had lost to the Population Police. Luke wanted to yell out, *No, stop! Don't tell me!* With each name he heard, he could imagine yet another person crowded into the room—ghosts joining the skeletons.

Eli finished the listing of names, and a silence fell over the room. Now that he had a little food in his stomach, Luke was thinking more clearly. He realized that he was the only one still eating, the only one who'd been given more than a crumb of bread and a swallow of broth.

It's just like the Population Police always said, he thought in horror. *If food goes to third children, others starve.*

Luke put his spoon down.

"No, eat," Adriana urged. "There is still hope for you."

"But do you think . . ." Luke had to be careful about what he said. "The Government always said that if people followed the Population Law, there'd be enough food for everyone. Do you think you're starving because some people broke the Population Law? Do you think illegal third children stole your food?"

The people all stared at him as if those questions had never entered their minds.

"We're starving," Eli said, "because the Population Police don't care if we live or die. And they made our lives so miserable, we stopped caring too."

CHAPTER SIXTEEN

By the time the "feast" was over, the sun had slipped down over the horizon, and the scene outside the windows slid into darkness. Eli began to talk of making a bed for Luke in front of the fireplace.

"You're welcome to stay here as long as you want," Eli said.

Luke's eyelids felt heavy as he watched the other villagers leave for their own homes. His legs felt so sore that it hurt just to shift position in his chair.

"Tonight," he decided. "I'll stay tonight."

Eli found threadbare quilts for him to sleep on. "Twila made this one," Eli recounted, laying the quilts on the floor. "This was Aileen's handiwork. . . ." He disappeared into a back room for a few minutes, and brought back a goose-down pillow. "Adriana wanted you to have this."

Luke curled up in the blankets. They were much more comfortable than sleeping on rock or decaying linoleum.

"Thank you," he said.

Eli didn't leave yet.

"There's a little bread left. Feel free to have some breakfast if you're up before us," he said, yawning. "You probably will wake up first. We spend a lot of our time now sleeping." He hesitated. "Good night."

Luke expected to fall asleep immediately after Eli left the room. But somehow his eyes stayed open. He stared at the embers of the fire, his mind racing.

What if the Population Police come back and find me here? What if they've figured out now that I was the one who dropped the gun and ran away?

What if the people in Chiutza are right, and the Population Police are totally out of power? Shouldn't the people in this village know that? Wouldn't it give them hope?

What is wrong with these people? Are they really going to die? How could they just give up like that? Why don't they send someone out to look for food? Do they truly want to die? Why?

Luke forced his eyes shut, but he felt no less alert. He squirmed around, the quilts bunching up underneath him. He got up and smoothed them out again, but he didn't lie back down right away. The moon had risen while he was curled up on the floor, and its silvery light drew him to the window. He stood there looking out at the bright, full orb in the sky, so much more beautiful than the dull, ugly huts of the village, the hard-packed dirt lanes, the leafless trees. And then he saw lights below the moon—a long string of lights along the lanes, snaking their way toward the village.

Headlights.

Luke jerked away from the window, dropping down below the windowsill just as he'd been trained to do when he was a little boy hiding in his parents' house. Then he realized how useless that action was, what a waste of precious time. Whoever was behind those headlights couldn't see him in the window from that distance. But they were getting closer.

Luke sprang up and dashed toward Eli's room. He banged his hand against the door.

"Eli! Adriana! Someone's coming! It's got to be the Population Police! You've got to run away! You've got to hide!"

An eternity seemed to pass before the door creaked open and Eli stood there blinking, his whiskers and sparse white hair in disarray.

"Didn't you hear me? We've got to wake the others! We've got to leave! We've got to hide!" Luke screamed. When Eli didn't move, Luke grabbed Eli's arm and tugged him toward the window. "Look!"

Eli stared out at the line of headlights. They were closer now, and Luke could make out vague shapes; he could tell which vehicles were cars and which were trucks. He thought maybe he could even make out the Population Police logo on the doors.

"Come on!" Luke said, yanking on Eli's arm.

"No," Eli said.

Eli's arm slipped out of Luke's grasp.

"Are you crazy?" Luke asked, spinning around. "Don't you know what will happen when they get here? You—you *defied* the Population Police! You said no right to their faces! They don't let people get away with that. Don't you see? They're coming back for revenge!"

Eli turned slowly toward Luke, his face still half in shadows.

"They can't do anything to us that we don't deserve," Eli said. "You run away—you save yourself. The rest of us will stay right here."

"That doesn't make sense!" Luke screamed.

Sorrow crept over Eli's face.

"I didn't tell you everything about our village," Eli said. "I was ashamed. You asked about illegal third children. . . . There was one in our village. Everybody knew. And we . . . we turned him in. We turned in his whole family. We informed the Population Police. And when they rewarded us, we informed on other people. Innocent people who had done nothing wrong except live next to us when we were hungry. We said they were rebels. We said they were plotting against the Government. We were like little children, tattling. We were that . . . gleeful. Only, the people we tattled on died. . . ." Eli was whispering now, his head bowed low.

"But—but—you saved *me,*" Luke said.

"One good deed, a million sins," Eli said, shrugging sadly. "Do you see why we would welcome an escape from our guilt?"

Luke backed away from Eli. He kept shaking his head,

wanting to protest: *No, no, you're good people, you were nice to me, you couldn't have sent anyone to their death. . . .* But Eli was looking back at the line of headlights again.

"You should leave now," he said. "You've got no part in our guilt. Here, take a quilt with you. And take our bread—we'll have no need of it."

Eli was rummaging through cupboards, shoving food into a bag. He thrust the bag into Luke's arms and wrapped a quilt around Luke's shoulders.

"If you go that way up the path, no cars can follow you," he said, pointing around the corner of the house. "They'd have to chase you on foot, and you'll have a head start."

Eli shoved Luke out the door, and Luke took off running, the food sack thumping against his legs. Every few steps he had to slow down and pull up the quilt so it didn't drag on the ground. Once he got into the woods it caught on branches, broke off twigs.

I'm probably leaving a trail, he thought bitterly. *I should just throw it down and keep running.*

But he feared that that would give him away too. And as he kept hugging the quilt around his neck, it began to seem wrong to leave Eli's gift behind. He remembered how tenderly Eli had handled the quilt, how sadly he'd mumbled, "This is Aileen's handiwork. . . ."

He also remembered how Eli had said, "We informed the Population Police. . . . We were like little children, tattling. . . ."

Luke was still close enough to the village to hear the

cars and trucks arriving, their engines rumbling and then, one by one, shutting off. He pressed the quilt over his ears because he didn't want to hear the screams and cries. But even through the quilt he could hear someone behind him shouting, "Wait! Stop!"

Luke veered off the path and ran even faster.

CHAPTER SEVENTEEN

Even with the moonlight guiding him, it was a nightmarish journey. Luke was in a section of the woods where the trees grew thick and close together. He couldn't tell the trees from their shadows. He ducked around trunks that weren't really there; he banged his head on too-real branches he thought were phantoms. When he tripped on a root and sprawled on the ground, he found he no longer had the will to spring back up immediately. He lay huddled under the quilt, listening.

"Lu-uke! Lu-uke!" someone called in the distance.

Was it only his imagination? Only the wind? Or was someone from the village trying to find him?

They probably want to turn me in, he thought bitterly. *They've changed their minds.*

He pulled the quilt tighter around himself, sealing off his entire body from the howling wind. He dozed fitfully, jolting awake every time he heard a noise. Then he'd lie awake in the darkness, his heart pounding, his ears straining to make sense of silence.

Someone's creeping up on me. . . . They're about to pounce. . . . He'd wait, but nothing would happen. *Nobody's there,* he'd try to assure himself. *Nobody's there at all.*

Finally he woke up to light. Even through the thick quilt, he could tell that the sun was high overhead now. The quilt was made of scraps of different colored material, and the effect was like stained glass, the cloth tinting the sunlight red and blue, yellow and green, orange and purple. For a while Luke lay still, marveling at the colors. Somehow he didn't care about being caught; he didn't worry about where he was going or where he had been. He didn't think.

Then the sun went behind a cloud, and the spell was broken. Luke lifted one corner of the quilt and peeked out.

Trees. Leaves. Sky.

He shoved his head out farther so he could survey his surroundings a little better. Then he burst out laughing.

This is perfect! It almost looks like I planned it!

He was at the bottom of a gentle hill. One whole side of his quilt—the side closest to the hill—was covered with leaves, blown there by the howling wind the night before. Anyone walking by would have thought he and his quilt were just a small hillock, a natural part of the woods.

I'll have to remember this trick, he thought, and that seemed incentive enough to go on, to have another chance to use such clever camouflage.

He stood up and shook out the quilt. He nibbled on a little of the bread Eli had given him the night before, then wrapped the food sack around his waist and the quilt around his shoulders. The sun came out from behind the cloud again, and Luke took that as a blessing of sorts.

I'm fine, Luke told himself as he took off walking toward the east again. *It's warmer today; I have food in my stomach. I'm safe. But it'd be nice to have someone to talk to, you know?*

He thought about how he'd felt standing with Eli and Adriana and the rest of the villagers. With their arms linked and their shoulders touching, they'd seemed so united. They'd had a common purpose. Luke had been much less terrified than he would have expected, because he'd had all the other people on his side.

Now Luke was alone again. And Eli and the others were—

Luke decided to think about something else.

Wonder who's taking care of my horses back at Population Police headquarters. Whoever it is had better be brushing Jenny down really well. It better not be some slacker who doesn't know anything about animals, like . . .

The image that came into his mind was the face of the boy who'd gone to Chiutza with him, who'd stolen Luke's cornbread and refused to share "his" territory with Luke. The boy Luke had last seen in the middle of a circle of threatening men. Luke couldn't see that boy caring much about horses, but Luke didn't want to think about him either.

What's there left to think about? Is there any part of my mind that isn't booby-trapped, laid with secret passageways back to thoughts I don't want to think?

Luke could imagine the kind of answer Jen would have given to that question: *No, there isn't, Luke. As long as third children are illegal, as long as we're not supposed to exist, you'll always feel trapped. You'll always* be *trapped. That's why you have to work for freedom.*

Luke wished Jen were still alive just so he could tell her to shut up.

The sun hovered overhead for a long time, then began to slip over Luke's shoulders, behind the trees. That was the only way Luke could gauge how long he'd been trudging forward. He tried to keep alert, to watch for any sign of Population Police officers or rebels with guns or even just ordinary people going about their usual business. But there was nothing to see. *Trees, sky, uneven ground—oops, watch out for that root over there. You don't want to trip again.* A couple of times Luke could see the edge of a field, just beyond the trees. Once he dared to detour toward the field, thinking he might find withered soybeans again. But this field, when he came to it, looked more like a meadow, abandoned to thistles and weeds. Luke could see the ruts in the field where tractor tires had once rolled. But it looked like that had been years earlier; clearly the weeds had replaced crops many growing seasons ago.

But why? Luke wondered. *Why wouldn't someone try to grow food here? People are starving. . . .*

Luke moved back into the woods, feeling more disturbed than he wanted to admit.

As sunset approached, Luke had a more urgent concern: water. His throat was parched after his hours of walking, and he hadn't come to a single stream or pond the entire day. The only water he'd seen had been dew quivering on fallen leaves early in the day, and he hadn't been desperate enough then to lick it up.

How long can someone survive without water? he wondered. *More than a day? A week?* He was too thirsty to remember.

Just as he began to despair of ever finding water, he saw a break in the trees ahead of him. He began moving very cautiously as soon as he caught his first glimpse of a house. *What if it's another place like Chiutza?* he worried. *Or what if it's a village the Population Police are in the middle of subduing?* His throat aching, he hoped for another abandoned village instead—one with deep, still-functioning wells.

And then, when he got to the edge of the trees . . . he couldn't tell. The houses before him were mostly shacks in bad shape, but both Eli's village and Chiutza had been full of broken windows and rotting roofs too. Luke squinted into the glare of the setting sun, reflected off dozens of windows. He couldn't see any people, but he could make out a bucket on a post, hanging beside a spigot at the back of one of the houses.

"Oh, please," Luke whispered. Did he dare? Now that he could see a possible water source, he felt half crazed with thirst. Dizzily, he crept forward, keeping his step light. If there were people inside the houses, he had to make sure they didn't hear him.

Luke made it across the entire backyard. His mind was playing tricks on him now, remembering the many times he'd crept from his family's house over to Jen's. He'd been in danger on those trips, too; he'd risked his life for something that wasn't even as essential as water. Or had it been? He'd felt so desperate to get out of hiding, to go outside. He'd needed the hope Jen gave him, the vision she left him with. Luke shook his head, trying to clear his mind. He reached out for the bucket on the post—and knocked it over. It clanged against the side of the house like an alarm, then plunged to the ground.

Luke froze. The sound of the bucket hitting the ground seemed to reverberate off all the trees in the woods.

But no one's coming. Surely there aren't any people here.

Luke dared to peek into an unbroken window. The house was dark inside. He could just barely make out an unmade bed, its surface a tangle of blankets.

See? Luke told himself. *Abandoned. It just hasn't been very long since the people left.*

Luke bent over to pick up the bucket. He was just straightening up when he heard someone behind him yelling, "Hey, you! What are you doing out there? Why aren't you inside watching, like everyone else? Come on!"

Hands clamped around his wrist before he had a chance to run.

CHAPTER EIGHTEEN

Luke jerked away, but the motion sent him into a fit of coughing. He doubled over, unable to run now.

The hands let go of his wrist and began pounding on his back.

"Hey, you okay? Here, take a drink—"

Through his coughing, Luke heard the spigot turn, the water gush out. He moved his head over and gulped the water straight from the faucet. He got too much at once and began to choke; then he swallowed hard and sipped at it a little more cautiously.

"I guess you were really thirsty," the voice above him said when Luke finally, weakly, took his head from under the water. Luke caught a glimpse of blue jeans, a sweatshirt, tousled blond hair—it was another boy, about Luke's age.

"Where'd you come from?" the boy asked. "Have you heard the news yet?"

"What news?" Luke asked.

"Then you haven't heard," the boy said. "Come on—you've got to see for yourself—"

He grabbed Luke's wrists again and began tugging. Luke could have pulled away this time, but he was curious. The boy didn't seem threatening; he didn't seem to want to hurt Luke. If anything, the boy seemed to want to help. Luke couldn't understand that, any more than he could understand why the boy sounded so happy.

No, Luke corrected himself. *He's not just happy. He's delighted. Overjoyed.* Luke wished his friend Trey were there to supply the proper word. And then Luke knew it: *This boy is ecstatic.*

The boy broke into a run, pulling Luke along with him.

They ended up at another house nearby. The boy raced in through the front door.

"Look, everyone," he announced. "Here's a traveler, wandering by, who doesn't know!"

Luke blinked frantically, trying to get his eyes to adjust. He could make out a whole crowd of people, all gathered around a television in the center of the room. Some of them glanced over at him, and he worried: *Oh no, I'm going to have to make a decision again. Which side are these people on? Is my shirt facing the right way? Should I turn it really fast to show the Population Police insignia?* Luke hugged his quilt tighter around his shoulders, hiding his shirt entirely.

It didn't matter. Most of the people only looked at him quickly and then turned their attention back to the TV.

"What's happening now?" the boy who had discovered Luke asked eagerly.

"Shh," several people hissed. One man added, "They're just showing—" but then he broke off, too mesmerized by the scene on the television screen to finish describing it.

Luke looked at the TV too. All he could see was a huge crowd of people, much larger than the one in this room. The camera panned past hundreds of faces, it seemed, all of them smiling or laughing or cheering. Then the camera pulled back, and Luke could see that the people were standing in a huge yard or field or meadow. Behind the crowd Luke could see the edge of a brick building.

His heart sank. He recognized the building: It was Population Police headquarters.

Luke had seen TV coverage of crowds cheering for the Population Police before. Last autumn, during one of the lowest points of his life, he and his friends had sat like zombies before the TV at Mr. Hendricks's house. For hours they had watched Aldous Krakenaur, the head of the Population Police, tell his vision of the future to adoring crowds.

"It's all staged," Luke's friend Trey had argued. "There can't be that many people who love him that much. They're probably being bribed to yell like that."

"Like, the louder they cheer, the more food they get?" Nina had said.

"Exactly."

Luke had wanted to believe Trey's and Nina's theories.

He'd never imagined that other people—people just watching the TV coverage, people who weren't being bribed—could stare as raptly as the people in this room were. Now he pictured people all over the country huddled around TVs, all worshipping the Population Police.

Then he heard what the people on the TV screen were shouting.

"The tyrants are gone!"

"We're free!"

"Liberty for all!"

"What—?" Luke burst out.

The boy next to him beamed.

"Isn't it great? The Population Police are out of power. The TV people say it was—how'd they put it?—a 'peaceful overthrow of the government.'"

On the TV screen, the camera zoomed in on two people holding microphones. One was a beautiful woman with long blond hair, and the other was a man in a T-shirt and jeans. *No,* Luke corrected himself. *It's just a girl and a boy. They're not much older than me.*

"For those of you just joining us," the girl began, then burst into a fit of giggles.

"Simone!" the boy scolded her.

"I know, I know," the girl said, flipping her hair over her shoulder and regaining her composure. "It's just, I almost sounded like a real TV reporter there for a minute, didn't I? All the real TV people ran away, 'cause they were scared, I guess. 'Cause they used to work for the Population Police, and they don't think they'd be very popular right now. So anyway, it's just me and Tucker here telling you all this, and Jacob behind the camera, of course—hey, Jacob, you're doing a great job."

"Come on, Simone, get to the news," Tucker complained.

"Okay, okay." Simone stood up straighter, serious again. "This is the official Population Police Network, Poppy News for short, except I think we're going to have to change that, because the Population Police are *over*. What do you think of 'Freedom News,' Tucker? Think that sounds good?"

"Simone, please, people are watching . . ." Tucker was shaking his head and grimacing.

"And they should be," Simone said, unruffled. "This is just incredible. This is a historic moment, one nobody would believe. I wouldn't believe it if I weren't seeing it with my own eyes—"

"We're at Population Police headquarters," Tucker interrupted, "where the people have taken over. They took back their own government—"

"Without fighting," Simone broke in. "No blood was spilled at all."

"Well, yeah, I think there was some fighting," Tucker corrected her. "Out in some of the villages. In the countryside. Some people are saying there were battles out there, and the Population Police just ran away. Because, you know, a lot of them weren't really into the whole Population Police thing, they just joined up because they had to, to get food. So that's what gave the people here the courage to take over the headquarters. Last night, I think, a lot of Population Police workers just left, so the building was practically empty this morning when this crowd showed up. They've been sharing all the food they found here—I had some really good bread, myself—"

"Tucker! You're not being very professional," Simone complained. "I don't think newscasters are supposed to say what *they* got to eat."

"But it's an important detail. The Population Police had lots of food here. They were living like kings when everybody else was starving," Tucker said.

"No more Poppies! No more Poppies!" Someone had started a chant behind Tucker and Simone. "No more Poppies!"

Simone started to say something else, but the sound was overwhelming. After a few moments, she just shrugged and held her microphone out behind her, to capture the cheers.

"Is this . . . real?" Luke asked, still in shock.

One of the men sitting in front of the TV actually glanced away from it long enough to answer.

"All the Population Police officials in our town ran away yesterday," he said. "That's real enough for me."

"And the Poppies wouldn't let something like that be on TV if they were still in power," another man said.

"But—who's in charge now?" Luke asked.

"Looks like Simone and Tucker are, don't you think?" the boy next to him joked.

Luke stared again at the chanting, cheering crowd on the TV screen. Simone and Tucker were clapping along now. Tucker spun Simone around, like they were so happy they couldn't help dancing.

"I have to go there," Luke said. "I have to see for myself."

"Oh, me too!" the boy next to him said. "I'll go with you!"

"Ricky Everts, you'll do no such thing!" a woman in the crowd burst out. "It's too dangerous. Any minute now, the Population Police could come back with tanks and guns and—and—"

"I'll take them," a man said, standing up. "It's like the girl said—something like this, you've got to see for yourself to believe it."

"Don, you're crazy!" the woman argued. "It's not safe—"

"I've been safe the last thirteen years," the man said. "Some things are more important than safety."

He began stalking toward the door.

Luke glanced back at the woman—Don's wife and Ricky's mother, he guessed. Her expression crumpled, and she held her arms out beseechingly. But she made no further move to stop anyone from leaving. Luke wanted to tell her that he understood her fears. *She's right,* he thought. *The Population Police do have tanks and guns. The people only have chants and dances. And hope. And . . . freedom?*

He didn't say anything to the woman. He just turned around and followed Don and Ricky out the door.

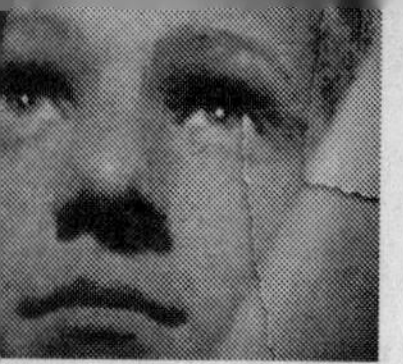

CHAPTER NINETEEN

By the time Don backed his pickup truck out of his garage, more than a dozen others had decided to join them. Don didn't seem to care.

"Hop in," he said, grinning from the driver's seat.

Three or four people crowded into the truck's cab; Luke was part of the group that jumped up into the truck's bed. He settled near the front, his back against the cab's window, his knees drawn up to his chest because there wasn't room to stretch them out. Most of the rest of the group were men and boys, though a few girls and women had crowded in too. At the last minute, just before they pulled away, Don's wife ran out of the house after them.

"Wait!" she called. "I'm coming too!"

"I thought you said it wasn't safe," Don teased her. "Did you change your mind?"

"No, but if you're going, I am too," she said.

The truckful of people cheered as she crowded into the cab. Two people got out to make room for her and scrambled into the back instead. Everyone scooted closer together to make room. As they drove off, Luke had one kid's elbow in his ear and another kid practically sitting in his lap.

"At least this way we won't get cold!" someone shouted, and everybody else laughed.

Luke couldn't help remembering another time he'd been crowded with a bunch of other people onto the bed of a pickup truck. That time, his brother Mark had been driving, and Population Police officers had been shooting at them.

Could those Population Police officers have just given up? Luke wondered. *And where's Mark now?*

Around him, people were singing as they sped into the dusk, giving the whole truck the feel of a traveling carnival.

"Hey, folks, I'm picking up the newscast on the radio," Don yelled back from the cab. "You won't believe this—it's Philip Twinings on the air!"

Luke was glad when one of the other kids asked, "Who's Philip Twinings?"

"He was a famous newscaster when we were kids," one of the men explained. "He disappeared after the droughts—everybody thought he was dead."

"Or arrested by the Government," someone else muttered.

"That's right—he spoke out against all the new laws they put in place. I bet he's happy now!"

"Be quiet back there and I'll turn it up!" Don yelled again from the truck cab.

The singing stopped. Dimly, over the rushing sound of the wind, Luke could hear a wobbly, old-man voice saying, "I want to thank Simone and Tucker for inviting me onto the air with them to cover this phenomenal turn of events."

"Don't mention it. We really didn't know what we were doing." Simone's voice sounded small and hollow, suddenly.

"You did very well. You'll be telling this story to your grandchildren someday, and you'll have every right to be proud," Philip said. His voice was stronger now. "We here at—shall we call it Freedom News, Simone?—are still trying to piece together this rapidly breaking news event. As near as we can tell, today's coup began with many small events. On Monday, the Population Police sent units out all across the country, to issue new identity cards. We've received reports that in many places, the people refused to be identified and some even attacked the Population Police units. And we've got an unconfirmed report that in Chiutza, a young Population Police recruit defied his commander and refused to shoot an old lady. He gave his gun to the rebels instead. . . ."

Luke gasped. He had to bite back the words, *Wait! That was me—but that's not exactly how it happened!* He looked around and was glad that no one was watching him. Some of the people around him were squinting off into the distance, as if that could help them listen better.

"Philip, no disrespect here, but that story is pretty

much confirmed," Simone was saying. "We had an eyewitness tell us that that's what gave his village the courage to throw the Population Police out. And everybody says that Chiutza is where the Population Police fell first."

Luke tried to make sense of what he was hearing. When he'd dropped the gun, could someone have believed he was turning it over to the rebels? Could his one action have made that much of a difference?

"Uh, Mr. Twinings, sir," Tucker was saying on the radio. "Shouldn't you say that this whole coup thing was caused by those rebels who destroyed all the I.D.'s? If they hadn't done that, the Population Police wouldn't have had to go out to Chiutza and all those other places to issue new identity cards."

Philip Twinings chuckled.

"It is indeed difficult to separate out all the roots of this incredible event. My guess is that historians will be trying to figure everything out for years to come. But just as there were many small erosions of freedom that led to the Population Police seizing total control, it would appear that many, many small acts of bravery brought the people back to power. Each act was important; perhaps the Population Police never would have fallen without every single effort. No matter how well journalists and historians do their jobs, the world will probably never know the full story of those brave acts or the total number of individuals involved. . . ."

A man near Luke was rolling his eyes.

"That Philip Twinings always was a pompous jerk," he muttered.

"Shh!" several others around him hissed.

Luke stopped listening so intently. He was picturing a glob of horse manure placed carefully in a path—his contribution to the effort to destroy all the identity cards.

Horse manure and a dropped gun—are you proud of me now, Jen? he thought. Maybe Philip Twinings was right, and even the smallest act was important.

Around him, the other people seemed to be getting tired of having to sit so quietly, listening.

"Shut up, Philip Twinings! I'm free to tell you that!" one man yelled, and everyone else laughed.

"No more showing identity cards every time we step outside!" someone else yelled.

"No more Poppies bossing us around!"

"No more Poppies telling us we don't deserve to eat!"

"No more Poppies!"

More laughter.

Luke could feel the edge of the Population Police insignia rubbing against his chest. If he told these people that he'd once been part of the Population Police, would they get upset? Would they believe him if he said he'd been the recruit in Chiutza who had maybe set off the whole overthrow of the government? Could he believe that himself? What if he told them he was a third child?

Am I still illegal? he wondered as he burrowed back into

his corner of the truck bed. He was still holding the quilt that Eli had given him, and he wrapped it tighter around his shoulders.

Illegal or not, he was still trying to hide.

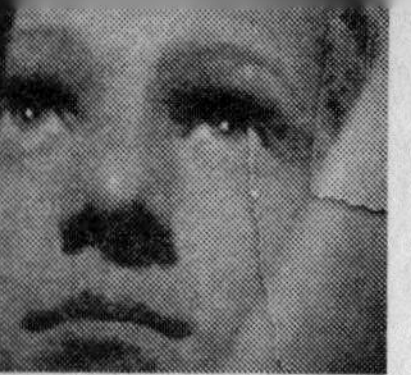

CHAPTER TWENTY

Dusk passed quickly into darkness, but that didn't stop any of the cheering and shouting in the truck. Luke wondered what the truckload of people would do if they arrived at Population Police headquarters and discovered that everyone had gone home for the night. *What would* I *do?* he wondered. *Where would I go?*

But when the truck neared the headquarters a few hours later, it was clear that nightfall had had no effect on the celebration. The gates stood open, completely unguarded. On the walls around the headquarters, someone had mounted huge klieg lights, so the scene within was as bright as day. Some people were dancing on top of the walls; others were cheering from the ground below.

Luke saw no sign of the barbed wire that had once surrounded the walls. He saw no sign of the guard station that had once stood by the gate—no, wait, there it was: toppled over and tossed to the side.

Don parked his truck several yards away, in the midst of

an assortment of other vehicles that people had apparently abandoned so quickly that some of them hadn't even bothered to close their doors.

"We're here!" Don called out, unnecessarily. "Everybody out!"

The others climbed down quickly, whooping and hollering and racing for the gate. Luke followed more slowly. He couldn't quite trust what he was seeing—his mind kept putting the barbed wire back in place, picturing the grim guards along the wall once again. The woman who had feared danger, Don's wife, hung back a little too. She gave Luke an uncertain smile.

"You never did tell us where you came from, did you?" she asked. "In all the excitement, did anyone even bother to ask your name?"

"No," Luke said. He didn't like the way she kept watching him. "I don't think names matter much anymore."

She started to say something else, but a crowd was shoving behind him, and Luke let the people push through, separating him from the rest of the group. By the time the tide had carried him to the gateway, he had lost sight of Ricky and Don and everyone else he'd ridden with in the pickup.

It doesn't matter. I've been alone before. And that woman seemed so suspicious.

At the gateway, the crowd bottlenecked, with people pushing from behind and everyone moving slowly at the front. Luke stood on tiptoe, trying to see what the holdup was. He had a quick flash of fear: *Maybe they're checking I.D.'s after all. Maybe this was just a trap, an elaborate hoax set up by the Population Police to catch people like me. . . .*

The fear didn't recede much when he saw the reason for the holdup: TV cameras. Simone and Tucker were interviewing people as they came through the gate, and even the people who weren't being interviewed were slowing down to gawk.

"We're not broadcasting this live," Simone was telling a thin, hunched-over man. "Philip is over by the wall doing the main broadcast right now. We're just creating a video archive that can be used later, after we edit everything. Philip says this will be like a historical document, almost. So tell me. Why did you come here tonight?"

The man straightened up a little.

"I came here," he began slowly, "because the Population Police beat me up when I asked for more food for my wife when she was pregnant. And she was pregnant *legitimately*. This was going to be my first child. She deserved that food. She needed it."

"Wow, sir—that's really sad. If you don't mind me saying so, you do still look kind of, um, scarred up," Simone said.

Luke could see the man's face now. He had a badly healed gash running from his right eyelid down to his mouth. His nose sagged, as though the bones and cartilage inside had given up.

The man stared straight into the TV camera.

"That don't matter," he said. "What matters is, my baby was born dead. Malnourishment, the doctors said. He—he would have been absolutely fine otherwise. So it's like the Population Police murdered my son. And I came to see for myself . . . if they really did have plenty of food here the whole time . . ."

His face seemed to break up along the lines of scars. It was a horrifying sight, until Luke realized the man was only sobbing.

"I just—had—to—see—," he wailed.

Luke stopped standing on tiptoe and turned away. He couldn't watch anymore. He kept his eyes trained on the gray sweatshirt of the man standing in front of him. He hugged the quilt around himself even tighter as he inched forward. Then suddenly there was a break in the crowd and a bright light shone directly into Luke's eyes.

"What's your story, young man?"

Simone's voice. She was standing there right beside him, holding a microphone out toward his face.

"Huh?" Luke grunted. He could see himself reflected in the lens of the camera, a caveman huddled in an old quilt, with dirt smeared across his face and twigs sticking out of his matted, messy hair. He looked back at Simone, and she was even more beautiful close up than she'd been from a distance or on the TV screen. Her waterfall of blond hair shimmered; her blue eyes twinkled.

"We're asking everyone why they came here tonight," Simone said gently. "What interactions they've had with the Population Police previously, why they're rejoicing now . . . This is your chance to tell the whole country your story."

Luke stared at Simone, too many thoughts tumbling through his head at once. He could admit that he was the one in Chiutza who had refused to shoot the old lady. He could say that he really hadn't handed the gun to the rebels—that he'd just dropped it and run away, so he didn't deserve too much credit. He could tell her about what he and Nina and Trey had tried to do at Population Police headquarters, how they'd persevered even when they'd gotten discouraged. He could tell about how his friends had rescued him from a Population Police holding camp. He could tell about seeing two people murdered, right on this property. He could tell about Jen, and how he felt haunted by her even now, nearly a year later.

He could talk about being a third child.

Then he remembered how the scarred man had talked about his wife: "She was pregnant *legitimately*." He remembered the woman back in front of the TV set arguing: "Any minute now, the Population Police could come back with tanks and guns and—and—" He remembered Eli talking about informing on the third child in their village. He remembered twelve years of hiding and watching his parents struggle with the fear that one day their secret would be revealed, that one day Luke would be killed.

"You—you're calling this Freedom News, right?" Luke finally said.

"Yes, that's right," Simone said. "We are."

She stood there expectantly, ready to record every one of his words, to broadcast his story out to the whole country.

"Then I'm free not to talk," Luke said. "I'm free not to tell you a single thing."

CHAPTER TWENTY-ONE

Simone stared at Luke as though he'd slapped her.

"Well, ex-*cuse* me," she said, flipping her hair over her shoulder. "You don't have to be such a party pooper."

Luke brushed past her and her microphone and camera and tried to blend in with the crowd. He began trembling immediately and couldn't stop. He felt as shaky and endangered as he had after running away from Officer Houk, from the Chiutzans, from the Population Police in the abandoned village, from Eli's home.

It's okay! You didn't say anything. No one's chasing you. Calm down!

He tried to focus on the people around him, to distract himself, to remind himself that everyone else was celebrating and happy. In the bright lights, their colorful clothes seemed to swirl around him, too intense to look at directly. Someone started singing what seemed to be a made-up song:

Oh, ho, ho
No more Poppies
They're all gone
We're so glad
Oh, ho, ho . . .

A group of teenagers was dancing along to the music, ending each stanza with an elaborate stomp on the ground.

"That's right! Stomp those poppies!" someone screamed near Luke's right ear. "Stomp them all dead!"

The screamer moved on, disappearing into the crowd again. Luke went from trembling to feeling dizzy. The colors and sounds blurred together. *Food might help,* he told himself, and he fumbled to loosen the bag still tied around his waist. He drew out the last crumbly crust of bread that Eli had given him and brought it up to his mouth.

"Hey, kid, you don't need to be eating *that,*" someone said beside him. "There's lots of good stuff up in that house. Free for the taking."

"That's okay," Luke mumbled, chewing the hard, dry bread.

Some of his dizziness subsided. He had energy now to shove his way through the crowd. *If I can just find Nina or Trey,* Luke told himself. *Everything will be all right if I find them.* Maybe Mr. Talbot and Mr. Hendricks had come to join in the celebration. And Luke's brother Mark might be there. And even his parents and Matthew. Everybody else in the entire country seemed to be crowded onto the Population Police grounds—why not Luke's family and friends?

Luke stumbled forward, looking right and left, pausing every few moments to scan the crowds cheering and dancing on top of the walls. When he'd first come out of hiding and gone to Hendricks School, he'd had a hard time telling people apart. One face looked pretty much the same as another to him, and he'd had trouble holding a mental picture of all the other students and teachers in his head. He had a momentary fear that a similar disorder might strike him now: In this crowd of strangers, what if even the familiar faces looked different to him, and he passed them by?

He reminded himself of what Nina looked like, with brown braids framing her lively features. And he could picture his parents' careworn faces, with wrinkles he'd memorized without realizing it. And Mr. Hendricks was in a wheelchair—how could Luke fail to notice a wheelchair gliding by?

He felt a little better, but he still didn't recognize any of the faces around him.

"Come on! Dance with us!" a girl called, reaching out and grabbing his hand. Luke pulled away.

"No, thanks—not right now," Luke mumbled, stumbling backward to get away from her.

He glanced past her and the other dancers toward the huge Population Police headquarters building. The first time Luke had come to this building, it had belonged to the Grants, the family who had donated his first fake name. Luke had felt terrified for most of the time he'd spent with the Grants, and he could still remember the panic that had gripped him when he'd returned to enlist in the Population Police. Now all the lights in the building were blazing, and he could see people passing the windows carrying food. They were laughing and hollering and cheering and dancing, just like the people outside on the lawn.

Where are the fierce Population Police officials who used to yell at us? Where's Aldous Krakenaur, the head of the Population Police? Luke wondered. Somehow he couldn't believe that all the top leaders would have run away, or given up so easily.

Luke's feet hurt, and the music and shouting were making his head ache. He wanted to find his friends, but he was so tired of searching. After he circled the crowd a second time without luck, he backed away until he found himself under an isolated tree, away from everyone else. He squinted up at the tree stupidly, trying to figure out why it looked so familiar.

Oh, yeah, he finally thought. He was back by the stables. This tree was one he had often faced when he'd had to stand waiting for inspection. He swayed dizzily, staring up at the tree. Then he turned around and crept into the stable.

The building was dark inside; evidently, the crowd hadn't made it so far back on the grounds. Or maybe someone had checked it out early in the celebration and decided it was beneath the crowd's notice. Luke stood just inside the door, inhaling the familiar smell of hay and horse. And manure, too—the manure smell seemed a little stronger than usual, probably because Luke had been away from it for so long.

"Hello?" Luke called softly.

A horse whinnied in reply. Luke was so sure it was Jenny that he threw caution to the wind and switched on the light.

"Hey, girl. Did you miss me?" he whispered, striding toward her stall.

But all the horses were watching him now, some of them whinnying loudly and banging their heads against their stall doors.

"Hey, hey, what's wrong?" Luke muttered. "Calm down, everybody—you'll have the whole crowd in here checking to see what's going on."

Some of the horses began rattling their feed troughs. The empty pans echoed against the floor.

"Geez, you guys are acting like nobody fed you today," Luke complained.

Oh, he thought. He remembered Simone in the TV broadcast saying that most of the workers at Population Police headquarters had left the day before. *They left, and nobody thought about the horses.*

Luke stared down the row of stalls—a dozen on each side, twenty-four altogether. He thought about how many stableboys had done the work of caring for the horses. His vision blurred a little. He stalked over to Jenny's stall. He pulled the pin out of the latch and swung the door open.

"There you go, Jenny!" he said. "If the people are free, the horses are going to have to be free too! Go find your own food!"

Luke stood to the side, giving Jenny free access to the doorway. Jenny stared at Luke, then dipped her head down and nudged her feeding trough toward Luke. The horse might as well have spoken. *I don't want to be free. I want you to feed me.*

"Didn't you hear me?" Luke yelled. "You're free! Free! Get out of here!"

Luke reached into the stall and gave Jenny a hard shove. Jenny balked, keeping her hooves firmly in place, right in front of the feeding trough. She raised her head again, looking pleadingly at Luke. Luke thought about how many times he'd been comforted by her gaze, how much sympathy she'd always seemed to carry in her dark eyes for his plight.

"All right!" Luke grumbled. "I understand! You're just a dumb animal. You've never eaten anywhere but in your stall. You don't know what freedom is!"

He shut Jenny's gate again and strode toward the back of the stable to get the oats.

It took hours to feed all the horses and clean out their bedding. But when Luke finally collapsed in Jenny's stall, on fresh hay he'd shoveled himself, he could still hear the music and cheering outside.

It sure seems like those people are free, he thought, pulling his quilt around him. *Why can't I be too?*

CHAPTER TWENTY-TWO

Luke woke up the next morning still in Jenny's stall. At some point in the night she'd lain down beside him, as if she were trying to guard him. Or hide him.

"You're not just a dumb animal, are you, girl?" Luke muttered, reaching out and stroking her neck. "We'll watch out for each other, okay?"

Luke got up and fed all the horses again. He was glad to have something to focus on, something he knew he had to do. But the sight of all the horses chewing reminded him that he'd had nothing but Eli's dry bread the day before.

Unless I want to eat oats, he told himself, *I guess I'll have to go on up to the headquarters building.*

That thought actually made the oats look appetizing.

Quit that, he told himself. *What would Jen say if she knew the Population Police were gone, but I was still scared to leave the horse stables?*

Remembering how filthy he'd looked reflected in

Simone's camera lens the night before, Luke took time to clean off his hands and face at the pump by the water trough. Then he threw caution to the wind and put his whole head under the rushing water, scrubbing at his hair with saddle soap. He traded his stained, ripped, inside-out uniform shirt for a long-sleeved T-shirt he found in a stack at the back of the stables where the officers always changed after riding. It wasn't as warm, but no one would recognize it as Population Police clothing.

When he was finished, he stood in front of Jenny's stall.

"I look a little more presentable now, don't you think?" he asked her.

Jenny whinnied and rubbed her face against his shoulder.

"Yeah, I know," Luke said. "Mother would be proud that I thought about washing up. But Jen would know that I was just putting off leaving. Hey—careful there with the oat slobber! I don't want to have to change my shirt again!"

He backed away from the horse's stall and resolutely moved over to the stable door. He opened it a crack and peeked out.

The sun was shining outside, and it was a beautiful day. Somehow it seemed that spring had arrived overnight.

Luke poked his head out cautiously so he could see around the corner of the building. The crowd was still there, out on the great expanse of lawn, but no one was singing and dancing and cheering anymore. People seemed to be talking quietly, some of them just now waking up. At the front, near the gate, Luke could just barely make out a figure with a camera on his shoulder and another person talking into a microphone. So the TV coverage was continuing.

Well, at least it doesn't look like the Population Police came back in the middle of the night, Luke told himself as he stepped out of the stable.

The walk to the main building wasn't a long one, but he had to step over numerous bodies in his path—people who'd been so busy celebrating the night before that they'd just fallen over right in their tracks when they got so tired they had to go to sleep.

Lucky for them it's so warm today, Luke thought.

He was glad that he could see their chests moving up and down—glad that he didn't have to wonder if they were dead.

If the Population Police really are gone, if everyone really is free—how long will it be before I stop thinking about things like that? Luke wondered.

He reached the back door of the headquarters building and let himself in. He was in an unfamiliar room lined with aprons hanging from hooks.

"The food's in here," someone hollered at him.

He stepped into a larger room, this one full of tables. It reminded him of the dining hall back at Hendricks School, but there were no cooks bustling about, doling out food. Instead, people were lined up in front of a long countertop stacked with apples and oranges.

"Yesterday there was made stuff, not just fruit," a kid

whined in front of him. "Where's the bread? Where are the waffles? Why aren't there doughnuts anymore?"

"All the workers left, remember?" Luke said. "Nobody's here to make bread or waffles or doughnuts."

But he wasn't thrilled about having just fruit for breakfast either. He circled the countertop and headed into the kitchen.

"Nina?" he called softly, remembering that this was where she had worked. He would feel so much better if she popped her head out from behind the row of stainless-steel refrigerators, or sprang out from beyond one of the long cabinets. But the sound of her name just echoed in the silent, empty kitchen.

I didn't really expect her to be here, Luke told himself. *She's free now, remember?*

He opened one of the huge refrigerators and saw stacks of egg cartons, enormous jugs of milk.

"Can I . . . ?" he started to ask, then shrugged. The Population Police were gone. Nobody was there to tell him what he could or couldn't do, what he could or couldn't eat.

Luke found a pan and oil and figured out how to turn one of the stove burners on. He hunted up a fork and a bowl and scrambled five eggs together, then poured them into the pan. The eggs solidified quickly, the clear parts turning murky white. The smell of cooking egg rose from the pan, taking him back in time.

Last April: my farewell breakfast. Mother promised the

chicken factory forty hours of unpaid work just to get two eggs for me. . . .

Suddenly he was overcome with homesickness, almost as bad as he'd experienced when he'd first left home to go to Hendricks School. He just wanted to go home again. And if the Population Police were truly out of power, that was possible. Luke's presence wouldn't endanger his family anymore. They wouldn't have to worry about hiding him; he wouldn't have to worry about being seen.

Luke flipped his scrambled eggs.

But who's going to take care of the horses if I leave? he thought. *And are the Population Police truly out of power?*

The eggs started to burn. Luke slid them out of the pan and onto a plate. He couldn't find any forks in the kitchen, so he went back into the dining room.

"Wow! Where'd you get that?" It was the same kid who'd complained about the fruit before.

"Made it myself," Luke said, feeling a little proud. "There's a lot of eggs and milk in the kitchen."

His words—or maybe the smell of the eggs, wafting through the dining room—set off a mini stampede. People rushed into the kitchen. Luke chuckled to himself as he sat down at an empty table and began to eat.

Just beyond the table, someone had wheeled in a television, hooked up with extension cords to a plug in another room.

"This is breaking news," a man was saying on the TV.

Luke recognized the voice: Philip Twinings, the newscaster he'd heard on the radio the night before. On the TV screen, he looked old and decrepit, with white, ghostly hair sticking out from under a tweed hat, and a white beard and mustache covering most of his face.

"Our researchers have been working feverishly through the night, trying to put together the story of this coup," Philip Twinings said. "This has been a most unusual event. History tells us that in most governmental changes, no matter how many people are involved, there's almost always one person who stands out, who leads the charge to strike down the previous regime. Until now, this coup appeared to be an instance of the will of the people overcoming a—am I allowed to say this now?—a totalitarian government. But now, we've uncovered the details of the plot behind the coup . . . and the mastermind who coordinated it all."

Philip Twinings paused, as if to give the people watching him a chance to gasp in amazement. Luke peered at the TV screen, and then through the window behind the TV. Distantly, through the trees, he could see the spot where Philip Twinings was standing in real life, in real time. The cameraman stood in front of Philip, and another figure stood beside him, though still out of range of the camera. Luke squinted. Something about the way the person was standing seemed familiar.

"We here at Freedom News have landed an exclusive interview with that mastermind, who's graciously agreed to talk with us now. I present to you—"

The camera panned away from Philip, then slid over to focus on the person beside him. Luke dropped his fork. He stopped listening to Philip. He didn't have to.

The "mastermind" was someone he knew.

CHAPTER TWENTY-THREE

Luke would have been overjoyed if the person on the TV screen with Philip Twinings had been Nina or Trey or Mr. Talbot or Mr. Hendricks or Nedley, another man who'd helped with their cause. He would have been proud; he would have stood up and shouted to the whole dining room, *That's my friend! I helped, too!*

But the person beside Philip Twinings was a muscular man whose face still sometimes haunted Luke's dreams.

It was Oscar.

Back in the fall, when Luke had witnessed the death of two people right in front of this building, Oscar had been the one who'd killed them. Oscar had tried to manipulate Luke, tried to get him to betray an innocent boy, maybe even tried to kill him, too. Before Oscar had slipped away into the darkness that awful night, some of his last words to Luke had been, "You're a good kid, even if you aren't ready to work with me yet" and, "You owe me now."

Oscar had always confused Luke.

And terrified him.

Now Luke peered at the TV screen, trying to understand. *Could Oscar have been involved all along? Did he help destroy the building where all the identity cards were stored? Did he coordinate the rebellions in the rest of the country? Have I been working with—for?—Oscar the past few months without even knowing it?* When Luke and his friends had first decided to go undercover to sabotage the Population Police from inside, Mr. Talbot had warned them about the need for secrecy. "The less you know about the other people you're working with, the better," he'd said. "If you are ever caught, God forbid, you wouldn't mean to betray your friends, but things might slip out . . . during torture. If you don't know much, you can't reveal much." So Luke had never known the fake names Nina and Trey were using at Population Police headquarters; he'd never known when or if his brother Mark had showed up to help; he'd never known anyone else's role in the plans they carried out. He'd been a cog in a wheel, and he'd never been able to see the whole wheel or where they going.

Could Oscar really have been the one steering?

"I must say," Philip Twinings was saying on the TV screen, "it's very courageous of you to step forward at this point, when there are still rumors that the Population Police haven't been fully, um, eradicated. For the benefit of our TV audience, I'd like to point out that Oscar Wydell is standing here at the former Population Police headquarters without any security around him."

"You're standing here without security too, Philip. You should be complimented on your courage as well," Oscar said, with a comfortable laugh. "I used to work as a bodyguard, and I learned to have a sixth sense about danger. I do not feel that I am in danger now. These are my friends here—my colleagues."

"I see," Philip said. "It's certainly been a very happy crowd, and everyone has been glad to find out about your role in the elimination of the Population Police. Do you feel that the overthrow is complete? Or are you concerned at all that the Population Police leaders might be consolidating their forces for a return to power?"

"Philip," Oscar said, leaning earnestly toward the camera, "I understand why people are afraid. Our country has been through a very dark time, ever since the first drought and famine nearly twenty years ago. In the past six months, the Population Police have achieved new heights of oppression. But one of the reasons I agreed to speak with you this morning is to assure the entire country that my people and I are in control. We have Aldous Krakenaur and the rest of his . . . his *henchmen* locked up in a secure location. In due course, we will hold a trial, and anyone who wishes to will be allowed to testify against them."

"And where might that secure location be?" Philip asked eagerly.

Oscar shook his head regretfully.

"I don't feel that I should reveal that, because of the extreme—and quite justifiable—anger so many people have against the Population Police," he said. "We will punish the Population Police through *legal* means, not vigilante justice. We plan to hold trials."

"But there are no laws in our country right now," Philip said. "There is no government. What standards will you use to try them?"

"The standards of basic humanity," Oscar said. "Now, if you'll excuse me, I have a great deal to accomplish this morning."

"Of course," Philip said, stepping back.

Oscar turned to go, the camera shot lingering on his muscular back. Then he turned back around.

"One more thing," he said. "What you've been doing, interviewing people about their experiences with the Population Police . . . That could be helpful, as we form our new government. We want to make this truly a government of the people. I have a vision of people standing right here, testifying, talking about the mistakes of the past and their hopes for the future. It could be . . . cleansing."

"What an excellent idea!" Philip gushed. "We've accumulated so much footage already, which we'll be showing momentarily . . ."

Luke watched Oscar disappear from the TV screen. Through the window, out on the lawn, he could see Oscar striding away from Philip and the cameraman, toward the headquarters building.

If he came in here, into the dining hall, would he recognize me? Luke wondered. *Does he know what* I *did? Would he call out, "Oh, yes, my brave friend, I'm so proud of you, so grateful for the part you played. Come and help us plan our government"?*

Would I want him to?

On the TV screen, Philip was introducing the footage Simone and Tucker had taped the night before of people entering the gates of the big celebration.

"Here's one of the more humorous responses we got," Philip said.

And then Luke saw his own image on the TV. Onscreen, he had Eli's quilt clutched around his shoulders and a desperate look in his eye.

"You—you're calling this Freedom News, right?" he was saying on the TV.

"Yes, that's right," Simone said. "We are."

The TV glowed with her loveliness, the camera clearly illuminating her lustrous blond hair, her bright blue eyes, her confident stance. Too quickly, the focus slid back to Luke with his wild hair, wild eyes, and ragged quilt.

"Then I'm free not to talk," the televised Luke said. When he'd spoken those words, he'd thought he sounded dignified and noble, like a legal citizen claiming his rights. But on the TV screen his voice came out squeaky, shifting from high to low ranges just in the course of six words. He sounded crazy. He sounded like he deserved to be mocked.

Luke blushed and slid lower in his seat.

Hiding again.

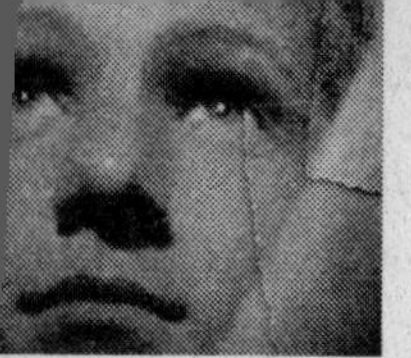

CHAPTER TWENTY-FOUR

The first time Luke had come to the Population Police headquarters building, when it was still the Grant family's private home, he'd spent a lot of time wandering around wondering who he was supposed to be and how he was supposed to act. After he finished his scrambled-eggs breakfast, he found himself doing the same thing. Before, he'd been plagued by servants watching him, asking him questions about his math grades and scolding him for not changing into his tuxedo in time for dinner. Everyone acted as if they knew everything about him, and he worried that they really did. He worried that they knew he was a fraud.

This time, no one seemed to take any notice of him at all. He was just another kid without an identity in a country full of kids whose identities had been erased.

"I suppose we can be anyone we want to now," Luke overheard a girl saying as he walked through the crowd outdoors.

"And we can *do* anything we want. That's freedom, isn't it?" the boy beside her said. He leaned over and gave her a kiss, dipping her down as if they were dancing.

"Or not," the girl said as soon as he released her. She wiped the back of her hand against her lips, as if she were trying to wipe away his kiss.

Wandering past, as good as invisible, Luke wondered if this really was freedom, this sense of being lost. A year ago, hiding, he'd felt like he'd had no choices; now he felt like he had too many. He could keep wandering, he could go back to the horse stable, he could go to Mr. Hendricks's house, he could go home, he could go find Oscar. . .

What's the right thing to do? he wondered.

Now that he'd seen Oscar on TV, heard him claim credit for the coup, Luke didn't feel like he could leave. In his mind, Luke kept seeing Oscar as he'd looked on the TV screen: powerful, confident, his muscles bulging, his hair slicked back. He'd been wearing a suit. Luke kept holding that image up against the way he himself had looked on TV, huddled in the quilt, his hair in disarray, his voice cracking as he tried to say, "Then I'm free not to talk."

Again and again Luke told himself, *Obviously Oscar has everything under control. It's not like he needs* your *help.* But there was always an echo in his mind, a tiny voice that asked, *But do you trust Oscar?*

Luke remembered how Oscar had told Luke that he'd been born poor, like Luke, and that he hated Barons, the people who had all the money. But Oscar had told Smits

Grant, who was a Baron, that he was a Baron himself. Luke remembered how little concern Oscar had had for Smits's fate, how calm Oscar had been when Mr. and Mrs. Grant had died, how he'd scoffed when Luke had asked if it was possible to fight the Government peacefully.

If I could just see what Oscar was doing right now, Luke thought, *then maybe I'd feel better.*

Luke turned around and went back into the headquarters building. He used the back door again, but this time he went past the dining hall, out into rooms he hadn't seen since the house belonged to the Grants. Back then, he'd thought of the house as an impossible maze, full of passageways that doubled back on themselves and rooms that didn't ever seem to stay in the same spot when he walked past. He knew the rooms really hadn't moved around; he knew the real problem had been his own fear and panic.

I've got nothing to fear now. I'm free, remember? I'm not trying to be somebody I'm not. The Population Police are out of power. Nobody's got any reason to want to kill me. I don't even have to talk to Oscar if I don't want to. I can just . . . watch.

The rooms he passed through were empty of the lavish furniture the Grants had once owned. Luke didn't know if the Population Police had taken it away, or if looters had carried it off after the Population Police left. Certainly nobody else seemed interested in these rooms now: Luke hadn't seen a single other person since he'd left the dining hall. Luke wondered about the contents of the filing cabinets that lined some of the walls, but when he pulled out the drawers, he discovered they were all empty.

Oscar said there would be trials, Luke remembered. *Maybe these drawers held records that proved all the crimes the Population Police officials were guilty of, and the records have been taken somewhere else safe, to be evidence.*

Somehow, though, the sight of all those empty drawers bothered him.

He moved on, looking for stairs. The really important Population Police officials had had their offices on the second floor, so it made sense that Oscar would be established there too. Didn't it?

Then Luke came to a doorway he remembered very well, and he stopped in his tracks.

"The secret room," he whispered.

Three times Luke had stepped through that doorway, each time with a different person. Three times he'd watched somebody type a special code into a panel on the wall, sealing off the room and making it soundproof and secure. Three times he'd sat in that room struggling to make sense of some new, devastating revelation. Once he'd held a key to the room in his own pocket, but he had no idea where that key was now. Too much had happened to Luke since then.

Luke was sure the door would be locked, but he reached out and tried the doorknob anyway.

It came off in his hand.

Luke gasped and looked around fearfully, as if expecting someone to yell at him. But nobody was in sight, and who would scold him for a broken doorknob when the whole government had fallen apart?

Luke put the doorknob back in its socket and gently pushed the door open. The room was windowless, and the lights were off. But there was enough light coming in through the doorway for Luke to see how this room had been transformed since the last time he'd been in it. The mahogany desk that had once dominated the entire space had been pushed to the back to make way for dozens of posters and signs stacked against the walls. One of the signs nearest Luke depicted a baby with the number three emblazoned on his chest. Luke moved the sign a little so he could see the words written below: HE'S THE REASON YOU WERE STARVING.

Luke turned away from this sign, and his gaze fell on another one depicting sullen figures with the words BEWARE THE SHADOWS. Another simply showed a woman and a man with two children playing at their feet and a third peeking out from behind the woman. The whole scene was stamped with a huge caption: THE WORST CRIMINALS OF ALL. Another sign, featuring a similar family, carried the words THEIR FAULT.

Luke sank weakly back against the wall and covered his eyes with his hands. He shook his head and moaned, "No, no . . ."

Luke remembered Jen telling him about signs like these. Propaganda, she'd called them. Lies the Government had made its citizens believe. She'd said there were signs about illegal third children posted at train stations and on billboards, in all sorts of public places. At the time, Luke had never been off his family's farm: He'd never seen a train station or a billboard; he couldn't imagine a public place. He hadn't even quite understood what a sign was. Since then he'd traveled between a very small number of places: his home, Hendricks School, the Grants' house, the Population Police holding camp, Chiutza. A small, tight circle of places, each trip taken at a time of shock and horror. He'd had no time to sightsee. He could have passed a million signs and not known it, because he'd always been too engrossed in the turmoil inside his own head. So he'd never felt the waves of hate that radiated from signs like these—hate that was directed at him.

No wonder he didn't feel capable of standing up again, of stalking out of the room and closing the door behind him.

These are old, he told himself. *This is just where the Population Police stored their signs when they were in control. But they're not in control anymore. They're out of power. These signs shouldn't have any power over me, either.*

Still he stayed slumped over in despair, surrounded by the signs' stark accusations, lost in his own fears.

Luke didn't know how long he sat there—maybe minutes, maybe hours. Even when he heard footsteps approaching the room, he didn't move.

Then he heard someone swearing and screaming out, "What is the meaning of this?"

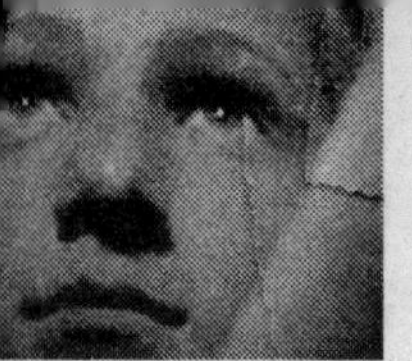

CHAPTER TWENTY-FIVE

The voice was coming from outside the room. Before he'd even quite registered the words, Luke's reflexes took over.

Hide! Hide! Hide! screamed in his brain, like an alarm system set at high alert. He thought about squeezing behind the mahogany desk, but it was in full sight of the door the angry person was about to walk through. Luke scurried to the darkest part of the room and weaseled his way in behind some of the signs leaning against the wall. The sign nearest him quivered and he got a horrifying vision in his mind: What if he knocked all the signs over and they crashed to the ground? He'd be discovered for sure. He reached up and steadied the sign, then yanked his hand down as bright light filled the entire room. Even from behind the thick layer of signs, Luke could see the shadow of dark shoes stomping into the room.

"Get me Melton," the voice was growling now.

The door slammed, and Luke jumped, his shock amplified because he knew the voice: It was Oscar's. Luke had heard that tone of cold anger many times.

"The point of putting the signs in here was that it was a secure, locked room," Oscar screamed. "That doesn't do any good if you leave the door hanging open!"

Oscar had to be speaking into a phone or a walkie-talkie, Luke thought, *because only one set of footsteps had come into the room.* Luke burrowed back tighter against the wall. There was no way he wanted Oscar to discover him now, not when Oscar was so furious.

The person Oscar was talking to must have protested, because Oscar was silent for a few seconds and then burst out, "Well, it was wide open when I got here!" Oscar seemed to be pacing, and when he got close to Luke's hiding place, Luke could hear bits and pieces of the other side of the conversation: ". . . key didn't work so I had to . . . really I did shut . . . nothing was disturbed, was it? And . . ."

"No, no," Oscar said, sounding a little calmer. "Nothing's out of place, as far as I can tell, and nobody was in any of the surrounding rooms. . . . I guess you're right; that's all anyone would think. And it looks like the security system is still working. Let's test the soundproof features, and then proceed with our plans if that's not broken. Who knows, maybe I can use this. Another bargaining tactic, you know?"

Oscar hung but kept pacing. Luke lay frozen behind the signs, his thoughts a panicky loop.

He'll find me. He'll get mad again. He'll blame me for the open door. He'll find me. . . .

But then Oscar moved away from Luke's hiding place and didn't come back. Luke heard the click of the door opening again, and more footsteps.

"Okay, we'll try it now. I can replace the lock later," another voice—Melton's?—said. "We won't have to move anything."

Luke could hear switches being flipped on and off, the door being opened and shut, Melton and Oscar walking in and out of the room, one of them murmuring, "Testing, testing, testing." Then Melton said, "You're good to go. Shall I bring him down?"

"Yeah. Sounds good. I'm just . . . I'll be ready." Did Oscar sound nervous? Luke wasn't sure what to make of that. In Luke's experience, Oscar never sounded nervous.

Luke's legs were going numb from being in the same position for so long. He dared to shift them ever so slightly, without rattling the propped-up signs. Now he had pins and needles pricking up and down his legs. But there was nothing he could do about that except wince and bite his lip and stay silent.

Luke heard more footsteps, but they stumbled, and there was an extra sound thrown in. The footsteps got closer—two pairs, Luke thought. And then they were close enough that Luke could recognize the extra sound: chains. Chains clanking and rattling and dragging on the floor.

Luke heard the door shut. The chains rattled and the chairs creaked as people sat down.

"I demand to be treated with more respect!" a haughty voice announced. "I am the supreme leader of the Population Police, I am in control of the entire country—"

"Not anymore." Oscar's voice, with a chuckle. "If you'll notice, you're sitting there in handcuffs and leg irons, and I am the one in charge."

"This is an indignity! This will not stand! Thousands of people are loyal to me—they'll come and rescue me; they'll restore me to my rightful position. And then *you'll* be—"

"They can't rescue you if they don't know where you are," Oscar said, his voice still light and amused. "And have you forgotten? Thousands of people hate you too. Thousands would love to kill you, to pay you back for everything you and your Population Police have done to them. A lot of those people are out on the front lawn celebrating right now. Want me to take you out to them? Want me to just yell out a window, 'Hey everybody, Aldous Krakenaur's right here. Anybody feel like visiting?'"

Oscar was standing up, probably walking toward the door. Luke wondered if this was what Oscar had meant by holding a trial, judging the Population Police by basic human standards. Maybe he was going to let the crowd in, let them decide what Aldous Krakenaur deserved.

Luke heard the clank of chains.

"Please, I beg of you—"

Luke couldn't see what was happening, but he thought

maybe Aldous Krakenaur had grabbed Oscar's hand to stop him. It was hard to hear over the rattling chains, and Krakenaur seemed to be whispering now. Luke heard the word "negotiate." He heard "negotiations" and "my loyal followers" and "loyal to you." But as hard as he listened, he couldn't make out a full sentence, a full thought.

"Well, yes, I suppose that could be arranged," Oscar said airily, as if he really didn't care. "With the code we talked about before—"

"Yes!" The way Krakenaur said that, Luke could picture him straining against his chains, still reaching out to Oscar. "They're true believers! They'd understand that!"

"And they would stay . . . loyal?" Oscar asked.

"Oh, absolutely!" Krakenaur assured him. "And then you could give me—"

"I'm giving you the opportunity to stay alive," Oscar interrupted harshly. "That's more than kind of me, I'd say."

"But after—"

"You've got no right to think about after. You should be thinking of new ways to be useful to me, so I don't decide to throw you out into the crowd," Oscar said. He paused craftily. "The door to this room has no lock—did anyone tell you that? It's one of those inconvenient little details that comes with taking over a building the previous occupants have left in bad shape. Just like taking over a government the previous leaders have left in bad shape . . . Maybe I should leave you in this room—blindfolded, handcuffed, chained to that chair. Maybe I should just leave everything to chance, to see if anyone happens to wander in here, happens to see you sitting there—"

"No!" The panic in Krakenaur's voice was almost palpable. "You need me! I can tell you where the extra food is stored! We have plenty of food!"

"That's a start," Oscar mused. "The rabble like food, all right. And they like me as long as I'm providing it. But I warn you—*I* want more than food. We'll just have to see if your promises pan out."

Luke heard Oscar's footsteps again, brisk this time. He stopped by the door and seemed to be shutting off the security system. Seconds later, Oscar opened the door and said, "Lock him up in the attic again, Melton. He's earned the chance to see another day. Get him to tell you where the food is, and have someone check it out. And then—come back and fix this lock!"

"Yes, sir," Melton said.

"Wait!" It was Krakenaur, pleading again. "You can't just—"

"I can do anything I want," Oscar snarled. "And you can't do a thing about it!"

Oscar's footsteps pounded out the door, followed more slowly by Melton and Krakenaur with his rattling chains. Melton turned out the lights and shut the door firmly behind him, plunging the room into darkness once again.

Luke lay still, blinking furiously, trying to make out shadows and shapes in the relentless dark. Even after he was sure his eyes had adjusted, he could see nothing but an inky blackness: no light at all. He strained his ears, listening to make sure the footsteps were receding, but the room's soundproofing evidently worked in both directions.

I've got to get out of here before Melton comes back and fixes the lock, Luke thought. *Before I'm locked in here forever—free and trapped, all at once.*

He crawled out from behind the pile of signs, his arms stiff, his legs' numbness giving away to pins and needles again. He tried to remember where each stack of signs had been, so he wouldn't knock anything down.

Nobody would hear you anyway, he assured himself, but there was a paranoid echo to that thought: *If I left a mess, they'd know someone had been here. Somehow they might be able to link it to me . . .*

So what? Why would anyone care? Oscar fought against the Population Police, just like I did.

Are you sure?

Luke stopped with that thought; he couldn't argue with himself and keep moving through the darkness at the same time. He inched forward, swinging his hands out in front of him. Finally his hand brushed a doorknob, and he grabbed onto it.

Go, quick, before Melton comes back! he ordered himself. But there was a competing fear keeping him from turning the doorknob: *What if someone sees me coming out of this room? What if they report me to Oscar and he figures out I've been eavesdropping? Or—what if they think I've got something to do with all those horrid signs? What if they blame me?*

Luke wished he had the courage to smash all the signs to bits before leaving the secret room. That's what Jen would have done. She would have smashed them and then waited until Melton came back just so she could tell him, *I did this. I took care of that part of the Population Police's evil. Let me go talk to Oscar, so I can tell him what I did too.* She wouldn't have stayed hidden while Oscar was talking to Aldous Krakenaur. She would have stalked out and declared, *Listen, I've got a thing or two to tell Aldous, myself.*

"I'm not you, Jen," Luke mumbled. But he managed to hold back the lesser of his fears and open the door.

CHAPTER TWENTY-SIX

Nobody stood on the other side. Luke glanced around once, then opened the nearest window and slipped out, pulling the window shut behind him. Standing safely on the ground, hidden by a row of tall bushes, Luke began to feel foolish. If nobody was guarding the unlocked room, nobody would have cared that he'd been in there. He could have walked out the front door of the building and nobody would have even noticed.

Luke fought his way out through the screen of bushes, emerging into sunlight and the same carefree, party atmosphere he'd seen the night before. People were dancing and singing again: "No more Poppies . . . all the food we want . . ." The crowd had evidently made up new words to the theme song since the last time Luke had heard it.

Nothing about the scene around him gave off even the slightest hint of danger or intrigue, but Luke's heart was still beating hard.

Oscar definitely seemed upset that the door to the secret room didn't lock, Luke reminded himself.

Stubbornly, Luke circled around to the back of the building again. A girl carrying a plate of biscuits opened the door for him.

"Want one? We've got plenty to share," she told him, grinning.

"No, thanks. Not now," he muttered.

He walked on through the dining room, where a huge crowd was singing as they crammed food into their mouths:

No more Poppies
All the food we want
We eat by day
We eat by night
This is
The greatest life!

From the other side of the dining room, Luke tried to retrace his steps through the maze of hallways, trying to follow the same path he'd used before to reach the secret room. Once again, the hallways and the rooms he passed were deserted.

See? he told himself. *You just overreacted after seeing those signs. Oscar was only worried about the lock because he wanted to have a private meeting with Aldous Krakenaur. And he had to meet with him because . . . because Krakenaur knows things that Oscar needs. Like information about where all the food is stored.*

Luke rounded the last corner before the hallway that led to the secret room. And then he stopped.

A man was leaning casually against the wall, turning the pages of a newspaper.

"Oh, hey, I wouldn't go that way if I were you," he said, straightening up a little. "They found some dangerous chemicals the Population Police left behind in one of those rooms back there." He tilted his head, indicating the direction of the secret room. "The new government's trying to clear it out but"—he shrugged—"you know. Better safe than sorry."

"Oh," Luke said. He hesitated. He was pretty sure the dangerous-chemicals story was a lie, and he wanted to keep going. But the man had his legs stretched out, blocking the hallway. Luke would have to actively shove past him. The man's stance seemed casual, but Luke suspected that his muscles were tensed, and that he was ready to push Luke back if Luke persisted.

"They asked me to warn people if anyone came by," the man said, shrugging again. "I figured it was the least I could do, given how much food I've eaten since I got here. You want some? I think someone was frying up doughnuts last time I walked through the kitchen. They ought to be done by now." He pointed off in the direction Luke had just come from. "Just go down that way, turn right, then left . . ."

"Yeah, thanks. Doughnuts sound good," Luke said, retreating. He looked back over his shoulder, and the man was still watching him. "I was really just trying to find the kitchen, but I got a little, um, lost."

He picked up speed, navigating the maze of hallways as if someone were chasing him. Or as if he were trying to run away from his own thoughts.

Those caught up with him.

Dangerous chemicals? Yeah, right, he fumed to himself. *That guy was guarding the secret room. He was just doing it from a safe distance so even he couldn't see what he was guarding. There was probably a guard stationed at the front door, too.*

But why are they guarding all those old signs? Are those supposed to be evidence for the trial, too?

And when Oscar met with Krakenaur, what were they saying about having negotiations and using a code? Why did it seem like Oscar was . . . bargaining?

Luke was passing through the dining hall again. He barely noticed when someone stuck a doughnut in his hand. He barely heard the song crescendoing through the room: "NO MORE POPPIES! ALL THE FOOD WE WANT!"

He stumbled out the back door, back out into the sunlight. To avoid drawing attention to himself, he went and sat down with the huge crowd forming near the wall, where Philip Twinings and Simone and Tucker were up on a stage, interviewing more people.

I don't know anything about how governments are supposed to work, Luke told himself. *Maybe that's just how things go when governments change—the new leader meets with the old leader, so they can work out lots of details.* He'd liked it when Oscar had been mean to Krakenaur, when he'd said, "If you'll notice, you're sitting there in handcuffs and leg irons, and I am the one in charge." He liked thinking about how Krakenaur was chained up now, hiding in an attic the same way Luke had had to hide from the Population Police.

Luke tried to remember how he'd thought and felt all those years he'd spent in hiding, when he'd known nobody but his parents and his two brothers—all those years before he met Jen and she changed his entire world. He'd felt powerless. Somehow he'd even understood that his parents were powerless too.

Krakenaur didn't act like he thought he was powerless, Luke thought. *He acted like he still thought he should be in charge.*

The rest of the thought came slowly. Just as Luke didn't trust himself to interpret people's expressions and body language, he had trouble reading between the lines of what people said and how they said it. He kept replaying the conversation between Oscar and Krakenaur in his head. Had Oscar sounded a little bit hesitant, a little bit awed, even as he threatened Krakenaur? Had Oscar been trying too hard to sound casual and unconcerned? Why had Oscar allowed Krakenaur to make suggestions, to bargain for his life?

Luke thought about all the times in his life he'd been bullied or beaten up: by his brothers, by other boys when he first arrived at Hendricks School, by the Population Police when he was in their holding camp. None of them had offered to bargain with him. They'd just punched him, kicked him, bossed him around.

As long as I was powerless, that is. As long as I wasn't threatening to tattle on Matthew and Mark, to bring in Mother and Dad. As long as the boys at school didn't need me to keep their secrets. As long as the Population Police didn't know I could escape.

Now, sitting in a crowd of very happy people celebrating the end of the Population Police, Luke felt a horrid certainty creep over him.

Aldous Krakenaur isn't powerless. He still has some control.

Over Oscar.

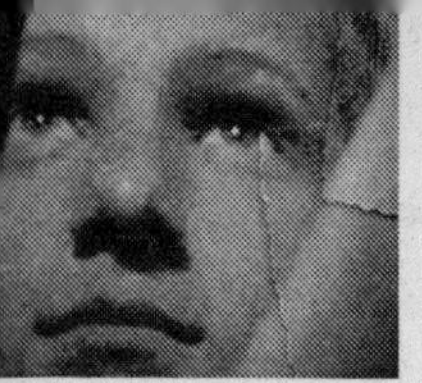

CHAPTER TWENTY-SEVEN

Luke turned to the people sitting around him. He wanted to tell them, *Listen—we're in big trouble.* But everyone else was clapping and cheering.

"We're back now, broadcasting live from the former Population Police headquarters," Philip Twinings was saying up on the stage. "We're ready to begin our accounting of the Population Police era. We'll be broadcasting as long as people are willing to talk."

The crowd cheered again.

They're doing what Oscar suggested, Luke thought, still horrified.

But what could be wrong with people telling their stories? What evidence did Luke have that Oscar was under Aldous Krakenaur's control? What could Luke do about it, anyhow? Who would listen to him?

Luke sat, paralyzed, letting the voices from the stage wash over him. A man talked about how the Population Police had refused to replace his grain when he accidentally spilled it. A girl talked about how the Population Police had confiscated the strawberries she grew in her own backyard. A woman talked about how much she missed her husband when he enlisted in the Population Police to earn food for his family. Luke started to relax a little.

This is just people telling how awful the Population Police were, he thought. *This won't bring them back into power. Maybe I'm wrong about everything. Maybe I misunderstood what Oscar and Krakenaur meant.*

He kept listening, the stories as soothing as a balm. The worse the horrors the speakers described, the better Luke felt.

Nobody would want the Population Police back in power after hearing this, Luke thought again and again, during tales of beatings, maimings, cruelty, contempt.

One boy painstakingly hobbled up to the stage, almost losing his balance. The crowd grew silent as they watched him slowly mount the steps, his upper body supported by crutches, his legs twisted and practically useless.

"The Population Police did this to me," he said into the microphone Philip Twinings held out to him. His eyes, caught in the bright light from the camera, were wide and terrified. He seemed to be having trouble breathing. "I joined up because my family was starving. They assigned me to shovel manure. I thought I was being . . . helpful. I suggested a better way to shovel, and they . . . they attacked me. I almost died. I would have died . . . if the rebels hadn't found me . . . if they hadn't fed me and nursed me. You can . . . look at me and see . . . what the Population Police did to our country."

He moved away from the microphone and began his slow descent down the stairs.

He worked for the Population Police shoveling manure? Luke thought. *He was in the stables, then. That's the boy I always wondered about, the one who asked for a bigger shovel. The one who disappeared. This is what happened to him.*

Luke watched the boy leaning down, lowering first his crutches, then the weight of his whole body, from one step to another. He seemed to be moving in slow motion, as if he didn't quite trust the crutches or his legs to hold him up.

He would be an ally, Luke thought. *He was in the stables with me. He knows what the Population Police are capable of. I could tell him about Oscar and Krakenaur.*

Luke stood up and began fighting his way through the crowd, toward the stage. The mood of the crowd seemed to have changed under the onslaught of sad stories. Instead of having people call out, "You there! Come dance with us!" or "Sing along!" the people Luke passed now muttered, "Watch it! You stepped on my foot!" or "Stop shoving!"

Luke ignored the complaints; he didn't want to waste any time finding the boy on crutches. When someone said, "Stop shoving!" he moved to the side and dodged around. But as he neared the stage, the crush of people began to seem impenetrable. Every time he tried to dart between people, the gap would suddenly close. He moved to the right; he moved to the left; he tried a diagonal approach toward the stage. Nothing worked. A line of bodies always blocked him.

"Excuse me," he finally said to a man who would not move out of the way. "I'm trying to get through."

"Nobody's allowed through," the man growled.

"But I'm trying to get to a . . . friend," Luke said, stretching the truth a little because it sounded so comforting to have a friend. "He was up on the stage just now. I want to talk to him."

"Nobody's allowed through," the man repeated, as if Luke had simply been too stupid to understand the first time. "We're protecting the people who go on stage."

Luke looked around and realized that the line of people blocking him from the stage wasn't just a random, accidental formation. These people were security forces. Bodyguards. All of them were tall and muscular, with stern expressions. They only needed black uniforms, and they'd look just like Population Police prison guards.

"Why?" Luke asked. "I thought everybody was free now."

The guard looked at Luke as though he were crazy.

"Would *you* be brave enough to go up there on the stage and talk about the Population Police, knowing that some of the Population Police officials are still on the loose? Knowing they might be out there in that crowd, hiding, even now?" he asked. "People are still scared. And they should be. Free doesn't mean safe."

"Oh," Luke said. "I guess not."

He stood on tiptoe to look past the guard's shoulder: He caught a quick glimpse of the boy with the crutches disappearing around the back of the stage.

"Look," Luke tried again, "I just want to talk to that kid over there. I promise I won't do anything to him. I wouldn't hurt anyone. I just—"

"Sorry," the guard said. "Rules are rules."

"But who made the rules?" Luke asked, trying not to sound desperate. "I thought the government was gone, I thought there weren't laws anymore—"

"Listen, kid, there's a new government now. Get lost!" The man shoved Luke away, and Luke's head slammed into the face of the person behind him; his body struck the shoulder of another man. This set off even more indignant complaints: "Ouch! You could have broken my nose!" and "Hey! Watch where you're going!"

"Sorry," Luke said. "Sorry, sorry, sorry . . ."

He struggled back through the crowd, to a vantage point where he could see where the boy with the crutches had gone. But it was too late.

The boy had disappeared once more.

CHAPTER TWENTY-EIGHT

Luke sat back down in the crowd again. He couldn't concentrate on the people on the stage, though, because his mind was racing.

It really doesn't matter that I couldn't get to the boy on crutches, he thought. *How did I think he would help? What could he do? What could I do? Maybe I just misunderstood what I heard. Maybe I'm just misinterpreting everything. What do I know, anyway?*

Around him, people were stirring angrily. Luke realized it had been a long time since he'd heard anybody clap or cheer. Periodically someone would shout out, "You said it!" or "I'm with you on that!"

Now everyone knows how bad the Population Police were, Luke thought. *They can't hide behind their own propaganda anymore. They could never come back into power.*

But that thought didn't cheer him. As he tuned in to the discussion on the stage again—a girl talked about how a Population Police guard had slapped her once; a man told about watching his son die of hunger—he took no more pleasure in the sad stories. The sorrow and despair and regret seemed to waft out over the crowd, infecting everyone. Luke saw several women crying. He thought about all the sad people he'd encountered since leaving home nearly a year ago: the frightened boys at Hendricks School, so desperate for a leader that they trusted someone who betrayed them. Smits Grant, who had to hide his grief over his brother's death. Mr. and Mrs. Talbot, who lost their daughter and had no way of knowing what happened to their two sons. The people of Eli's village, who lost their homes and their dignity and their will to live.

"That's wrong! Just wrong!" the people around Luke were shouting now.

"It's not enough to be free," a man on the stage was saying. "We must also have revenge."

"You tell it!" a woman shouted behind Luke.

"Yes!" erupted from elsewhere in the crowd.

The man waited for the jeers and whoops to diminish. He held up his hand for silence.

"And yet . . ." he said slowly, and the words seemed to hang in midair. Some of the people around Luke were listening so closely for the man's next words that they seemed to be holding their breath.

"I don't believe any of this was the Population Police's fault," the man finished.

Luke expected the crowd to explode with outrage. Of course it was the Population Police's fault! Who else had controlled the food supply? Who else had paid the salary of the guards who slapped young girls, who beat young boys until they could barely walk?

But the crowd stayed silent. They waited for the man's next words.

"The Population Police promised my village a food shipment last month," the man said, his voice hushed. Luke had to strain to hear. "They were eager to send it to us; they were happy to provide. They had no reason to want us to suffer. But the day came for the shipment to arrive and . . ." The man held out his empty hands, palms up. "Nothing. We called Population Police headquarters. The food had been sent, right on schedule. The reason we never received it? It was stolen."

The crowd gasped. Somewhere near the back, a lone voice cried out, "Who stole it?"

The man was shaking his head, overcome with sorrow. He buried his face in his hands for a moment, trying to regain his composure. Then he raised his head again and stared out at the crowd.

"Illegal third children," he said. "A band of them swept out of the fallow fields, attacking the trucks of food. They were like bandits, preying on innocent citizens, stealing innocent citizens' food. *That* is why the Population Police had to become so harsh, why they had to crack down so cruelly. *That* is why the food they promised us never showed up. *That* is why the Population Police never got a chance to govern as they wanted."

Boos and hisses began to spill out of the crowd.

"This guy is crazy," Luke said to the man sitting next to him, who seemed to be booing particularly loudly.

"What do you mean?" the man said, shooting Luke a nasty look. "He's the first person I've heard talk sense."

"He's the first person who's said *why* the Population Police failed," another man said.

Then Luke heard the boos and hisses differently. They weren't directed at the man on the stage. They weren't directed at the Population Police. They were directed at third children.

They were directed at *him.*

"Boo, illegals!"

"Blame the illegals!"

"It's their fault! It's their fault!" the crowd began to chant.

The two men sitting near Luke kept looking at him, because he wasn't joining in the chant. He scrambled to his feet and backed away from them. The boos were ringing in his ears. He tried to run, but the crowd was packed too closely together: He bumped into elbows, hips, shoulders, knees.

And then, out of breath and panting with panic, he reached the back of the crowd.

"Well, uh, we have another speaker coming up now," Philip Twinings was saying into his microphone, trying to regain control of the crowd. "Perhaps he'll have a different perspective."

Luke turned around, feeling one last glimmer of hope.

He had to feel hopeful, because the only other alternative was to give up, to give in to despair.

So the Population Police are out of power and I'm still illegal? he wondered. *It's still all my fault that people starve?* He remembered how devastated he'd been all those months ago, when Jen had explained the reason for the Population Law. Back then, he'd had to struggle so hard to believe that the law was wrong, that he still had a right to exist.

He watched another man step up to the microphone.

"I met an illegal third child, once," he said. "It was hardly human, I'd say. It stole food every chance it got. It—"

The man kept talking, but Luke couldn't hear him anymore. The microphone seemed to have given out.

Philip Twinings took the microphone from the man.

"We—," he shouted, and the microphone came back on for one brief moment, in a screech of feedback. "We seem to be having some technical difficulties. We'll break for the night and resume in the morning."

Luke hadn't even noticed that it was dusk now, that a full day had passed while he'd been sitting there in the crowd listening to stories. Around him in the hovering darkness, people were standing up, breaking out of their trances. Most of them were grumbling about being hungry, and they began streaming back toward the main building, heading for the kitchen and dining room.

Luke was hungry too. He hadn't eaten anything since the scrambled eggs that morning. He could remember being handed a doughnut after he'd discovered the man guarding the secret room, but he'd been too distracted to bring the doughnut up to his mouth, to chew, to swallow. Maybe he'd dropped the doughnut; maybe someone had taken it from his hand and he hadn't even noticed. He looked wistfully toward the bright lights coming from the dining-room windows. He could imagine hot soups, toasty breads. But there was no way he could join the crowd getting food. Not now.

Hungry and cold, Luke stomped back to the stable and fed the horses. He found his quilt still in Jenny's stall and he curled up in it.

"It was just two men talking bad about third children. Nobody else mentioned us," he whispered to Jenny. She turned around and looked at him with her sympathetic horse eyes, but she didn't stop chewing her oats. Even in the dim light of the stable, Luke could see her strong teeth chomping the oats to bits.

"Maybe it wasn't really that many people in the crowd booing," he told the horse. "Maybe it just seemed like a lot because I was scared. And everybody still hates the Population Police. As long as they hate the Population Police, I'm okay."

Jenny seemed to have a skeptical look on her face, but what did she know? She was just a horse chewing oats. Luke closed his eyes and burrowed deeper into the straw, which he'd neglected to clean. He didn't care. He slipped into a fitful sleep and immediately began to dream: Jen was there, and she was yelling at him.

Luke! Wake up! You've got to wake up!

It's nighttime. Supposed to . . . sleep . . . in the nighttime, he mumbled back in the dream. He curled up even more tightly in his quilt cocoon.

No, Luke! I mean it! Jen screamed again. *WAKE UP!*

She began tugging on the end of his quilt, trying to spin him out of it. And then he did wake up a little, just enough to realize that Jenny the horse was standing on one corner of the quilt, the force of her weight pulling it away from Luke.

"Hey, girl," Luke muttered sleepily. "Whose side are you on, anyway?"

He yanked the quilt away and fell back asleep.

When he woke up for real, hours later, sunlight was streaming in through the skylights, but he felt cold, stiff, and lightheaded with hunger. He hadn't had Jenny's body heat to warm him: The horse was standing against the wall at the other end of the stall.

"What? Are you mad because I didn't clean your stall last night?" Luke asked. "Or were you listening to those speeches yesterday? Don't tell me you blame third children for everything too."

His voice caught a little; this morning he wasn't even capable of making a stupid joke to a dumb old horse. Jenny just stared at him, in the steady way of horses, and he thought he heard an echo of his dream: *Luke! I mean it! WAKE UP!*

"I've got to get something to eat before I go totally nuts," Luke muttered to himself.

He put out food for the horses again, scrubbed his face, changed his clothes. By the time he stumbled out of the stable, he felt better. The warnings of nightmares and ghosts seemed silly in the glare of such a bright, sunlit day.

He started to veer toward the kitchen and dining hall immediately, but he could hear the boom of amplified voices off in the distance. Philip Twinings and the other TV people must have managed to fix the microphone and whatever else was broken. Luke could tell by the crowd gathering on the lawn that the interviews were beginning again.

I'll just go listen to a speech or two, Luke told himself. *Just to make sure . . .*

As he moved toward the crowd, he could tell that more had changed overnight than just a microphone repair. Someone had posted signs along the wall behind the stage, in full sight of the entire crowd and anyone who might be watching on TV. Luke began walking more slowly, each step filled with dread. Finally he was close enough to read the signs.

One showed a baby with a number three on his chest, with a caption underneath: HE'S THE REASON YOU WERE STARVING.

Another showed a sullen group of teenagers, with the words BEWARE THE SHADOWS.

Others showed families with three children. They were labeled THE WORST CRIMINALS OF ALL and IT'S ALL THEIR FAULT.

They were the signs from the secret room.

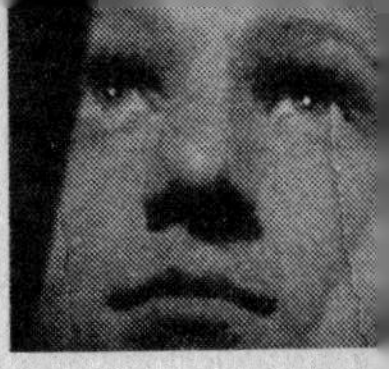

CHAPTER TWENTY-NINE

It took every ounce of self-control Luke possessed not to scream out, *NOOOOOO . . .*, not to run up to the wall and tear down every single sign, one after the other. As it was, he made a kind of whimper, deep in his throat, and suddenly all the people around him were peering at him suspiciously.

"Sorry," Luke muttered. "I'm . . . It's . . . nothing. Don't mind me."

He turned and fled, back to the stable, back through the door, back into Jenny's stall. He threw his arms around her neck and buried his face against her hide.

"It doesn't matter," he muttered into her mane. "Even if I tried to tear down those signs, the guards would stop me. They'd lock me up. Just like the Population Police would. Nothing's changed."

He was just talking, complaining, all but crying into Jenny's mane. But was it true? Had nothing changed? Even with the Population Police gone?

Luke thought about how the signs looked, all glossy and bright, the colors gleaming in the sunlight. They didn't look like signs that had been lying around in a dusty storeroom, left over from an old regime. They looked brand-new.

What if they hadn't belonged to the Population Police? What if they'd been created on someone else's orders? Like . . . Oscar's?

Luke's grasp on Jenny's neck began to slip. She shook her mane and nudged against him, as if she were nudging him to think some more.

"Maybe that's why Oscar was trying to protect the signs," Luke whispered. "Maybe he doesn't care at all about evidence against the Population Police. Maybe he just . . ."

Luke stumbled back from Jenny and slammed against the stable wall, staggered by the force of what he'd just figured out.

"Oh, no . . . oh, no . . . What if this is the code Oscar was talking about?" he cried out in a strangled voice he barely recognized as his own.

He remembered the few words he'd heard Krakenaur whisper to Oscar, during the only part of the conversation Luke hadn't been able to hear completely: "my loyal followers" and "loyal to you." Some code was supposed to make Krakenaur's followers switch their allegiance to Oscar.

"They're true believers," Krakenaur had said. "They'd understand that."

What would Krakenaur's followers understand better than hating third children?

Luke slumped down to the floor, his chin thudding against his knees, horrible realizations flooding over him. He hadn't been able to understand anything for the past twenty-four hours; now he didn't want to. He saw all too clearly how everything worked. Aldous Krakenaur had been overthrown, but Oscar wanted Krakenaur's old followers—the other Population Police officials—to follow him instead. Maybe he didn't think he could keep control without them. That was why he'd been willing to negotiate with Krakenaur. So Oscar and Krakenaur had agreed on a signal to let the Population Police officials know that Oscar wasn't completely against them, that he'd still let them have some power if they supported him. And the signs could do that, making them think Oscar hated third children too.

Does he? Luke wondered. *Does he really think third children are the reason people starved?*

Luke remembered how easily Oscar had lied about being a Baron, how he had managed to convince both Luke and Smits that he was on their side.

Oscar doesn't care, Luke thought. *He doesn't care if third children are the enemy or not, just as long as blaming them helps him. He's like the boy back in Chiutza, who didn't really believe anything, who chose sides based on who would fill his belly.*

Luke picked at the straw beneath his feet, tearing the shafts apart down to their hollow core.

It's probably not even real to Oscar. It's probably just a code to use. But real people are going to be hurt.

Jenny whinnied anxiously, as if it bothered her to see Luke slumped over in the muck.

"What do you care? You're just a horse," Luke muttered. "You didn't even want to be free when I opened your gate. I do. I've wanted freedom ever since Jen told me what it was. And now everyone else is free. But I'm not. Third children aren't ever going to be free."

He kicked at the muck, his despair giving way to anger. A glob of manure flew up and hit Jenny in the leg. She whinnied again.

"I know, I know—it's not your fault. Sorry, girl," Luke apologized. "But what else am I supposed to do?"

Stop Oscar. It was like Jen's ghost was back again, talking in Luke's head. *Stop him before he has total control.*

"Oh, yeah, right. And how am I supposed to do that?" Luke had a vision of himself hunting Oscar down, tapping him on the shoulder, then mumbling, *Hey, would you mind using some other code to attract your followers? The whole third-child theme hits a little close to home for me. Okay?* And then he could picture Oscar punching him, casting him aside, throwing him into prison for the rest of his life.

Out loud, Luke moaned, "The Population Police were right about one thing. I am just a worthless stableboy, wallowing in the muck. I can't do anything."

You're not worthless. Nobody's worthless. Do what I did.

It was Jen's voice in his head again.

"What, get myself killed?" Luke muttered bitterly.

No! I mean, you should go public with this.

Luke could have argued with that, too. He could have complained that Jen had planned her rally for months, while he had no time at all. He could have mentioned that she had had forty others marching with her, while he had no one: He was alone except for a horse and the ghost he argued with in his head. He could have pointed out that even with all her preparation, all her planning, all her calculations, and all her supporters, her rally had still been a tragic failure.

But the word "public" had given him an idea. Maybe, just maybe . . .

Luke stood up and brushed off the straw sticking to his clothes. He took a deep breath, then walked out of the stall, out of the stables, back out to the crowd gathered around the stage. He positioned himself carefully near a group eating muffins in the sunshine. The group consisted of three men and two women, and none of them seemed to be paying much attention to the people speaking up on the stage. One of the women was licking butter off her fingers. One of the men was demonstrating how he could toss a muffin in the air and catch it in his mouth.

Luke steadied himself with another deep breath.

Not everybody in the crowd was booing third children last night, he told himself. *Not everybody joined in the chant.*

"Hi," he said, forcing himself to smile and make eye contact with all five muffin-eaters.

"Want some?" the woman with the butter on her fingers asked. "We got extra, and if I have to watch Boris catch another muffin in his mouth, I think I'm going to be sick."

"Thanks," Luke said, taking one of the muffins she held out to him. He bit into it, but he was too nervous to really taste it. "This is all kind of weird, don't you think? I mean, all those signs that somebody put up overnight. Don't they look like what the Population Police tried to make us believe? I thought the Poppies were *gone*."

All five muffin-eaters looked at him doubtfully.

"Well . . ." one of the men said finally. "Those people up on stage have been saying the Population Police were kind of unfairly accused. Framed, you know? A lot of things we blamed them for, it was really the illegals' fault. I reckon if they're allowed to say that up on stage, and on TV and everything, there must be some truth to it."

"But the Population Police said lots of things on TV that weren't true!" Luke protested.

The muffin-eaters were all staring at him now. His voice had maybe soared a little too high, sounded a little too bitter.

"We don't really know that, do we?" one of the other men said. "It's hard telling what was going on, with all those illegals running around stealing things."

"I know one thing," the woman with the buttery fingers said with a shrug. "These muffins are real good. Those people can talk all they want to up there, as long as they're giving us all this great food."

The rest of the group nodded agreement, and Boris popped another muffin into his mouth.

"But where did the food come from? Who's providing it? Who put those signs up? And how can you possibly believe—" Luke broke off, because his voice was arcing toward hysteria. He panted, trying to regain control of himself.

"You ask too many questions," the woman said, looking like she regretted offering him any of their food. "Go away. You're bothering us." She turned her back on him. The rest of the group glared at him until he backed away.

They're just five people, and there are hundreds of others here, Luke told himself. *Try somebody else.*

For the next few hours, Luke went from person to person, from group to group. Some people shoved him away angrily; others just shrugged and ignored him. Only a few bothered to listen, and even they seemed to be keeping one ear on the rants from the stage, even as Luke whispered, "It doesn't make sense, does it? How many third children could there be in the whole country? They were illegal—how could they have had so much power over the entire Population Police?"

It took such courage for Luke to approach yet another person after each rejection. Meanwhile, up on the stage, the rants were becoming more rabid.

"The Population Police wanted to do their best for the people of our nation. The illegals only thought about themselves. . . ."

"Every third child must have been born with an extra gene for greed . . . for lawlessness . . . for hate. . . ."

"If only we could rid our country of the illegals once and for all . . ."

Finally Luke sagged in despair against a tree trunk. Even if people listened to him, he could reach only a few at a time, while the speakers on the stage spewed their hatred at the entire crowd—and the entire country through the TV broadcast. It was like Luke was in a sinking ship, with water pouring in through dozens of holes, and all he had to bail with was a teaspoon.

You'll have to go up on the stage yourself then, Jen's ghost argued in his head. *Tell everybody what you have to say.*

"Noooo," Luke moaned. He couldn't do that. There was no way he could stand in front of all those people, all those cameras.

Then you'll let them turn the whole crowd against third children all over again, once and for all? You'll let Oscar and Aldous Krakenaur win? You're willing to go back into hiding, to cower in an attic the rest of your life? That is, if they don't find you, if they don't kill you and your entire family . . .

"All right!" Luke snapped, and he knew he looked like a total lunatic, standing by a tree arguing with empty air.

Before he could let himself change his mind, he shoved his way back into the crowd, back toward the stage. This time when he reached the line of security guards blocking the stage, he said, very fast before he lost his nerve, "Please-you-have-to-let-me-through-I-want-to-be-one-of-the-speakers-on-the-stage."

The security guard standing before him laughed.

"You think you can just waltz up there, just like that? We've got a three-day backlog of people waiting to talk. You really think you've got something to say that anyone wants to hear? You go over there, talk to those people. They'll interview you, decide if you've got anything worth saying."

The guard pointed over to a table set up in the building that used to be the Population Police garage. Behind the table sat three men, who stared out cold-eyed at the crowd. Luke recognized all three of the men. They used to come into the stables when he worked there, asking for the very best horses.

All of them had once been Population Police officials.

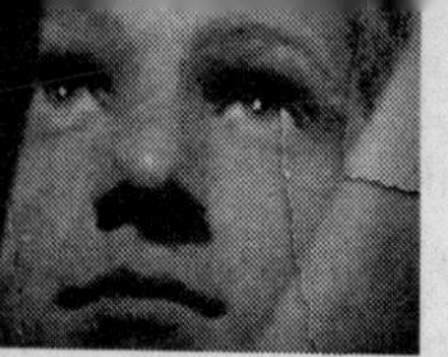

CHAPTER THIRTY

Luke backed away from the security guard in horror. The guard was still sneering, his mouth wide and distorted, his teeth glistening and sharp. Luke turned and fled, shoving his way back through the crowd. For the second time that morning, he raced back to the stables, desperately seeking a safe haven from his fears. His hands shook as he unlatched the door to Jenny's stall. This time he simply flung himself onto the floor of her stall, not caring about the straw, not caring about the muck. What was there left to care about anymore?

Jenny whinnied anxiously and nudged his back with her nose.

"It's all a setup," Luke mumbled. "It always was. The people talking on stage—they're signaling all the rest of the old Population Police officials. They're brainwashing the crowd. It's all very carefully controlled. They'd never let me up there."

Luke remembered how he'd thought he was safe as long

as the crowd hated the Population Police. He hadn't realized how easily hate could be spread, how easily it could be turned toward a new target. With three more days of speeches, the crowd would be ready to burn third children at the stake. They wouldn't care how many former Population Police officials helped them do it.

Jenny nudged him again, as if she were trying to make him get up.

Luke rolled over on his back.

"Forget it. I'm not going anywhere," he told her. "I'm giving up. There's nothing I can do."

Jenny whinnied once more, and shoved her head against the door to her stall. Luke saw that he'd neglected to latch the door after he'd rushed in.

"What? Is that bothering you?" Luke asked harshly. "You scared you might actually have a little freedom? Scared you might have to make some choices?"

His eyes blurred as he remembered how thought he'd been free too, only the day before, and how he'd worried that freedom meant having too many choices. Now he didn't feel like he had any.

"Okay, okay, I'll fasten that," Luke told Jenny. "It wouldn't be fair for a horse to have more freedom than I do."

But as he stood up, Jenny moved away from him. She nudged her gate open and stepped out of her stall. Maybe it was all Luke's imagination, or maybe it was just a trick of the eye in the dim light of the stable, but she seemed to look back at him with a mixture of wonder and hope in her eyes.

"Hey, girl, don't go too far," Luke said. "It probably wouldn't be safe for you to go out and mix with the crowd. They're not in a very friendly mood."

Yet he could imagine the horse stepping daintily through the crowd, unscathed. Even fired up by the speeches, even filled with hate, surely the crowd would be able to look at Jenny with awe, to see the beauty in her stride.

And then, strangely, he began to imagine himself on Jenny's back, riding across the lawn. He saw the crowd falling silent, the speeches cut off, everyone watching him and Jenny. He pictured Jenny leaping . . . He gasped.

"Do you think we could?" he asked Jenny hoarsely. "Do you suppose that's the way to . . . ?"

He played the scene over and over again in his head. Somehow it mixed with other scenes and sounds he had witnessed. He saw the woman back in Chiutza staring him in the face and declaring, "I have a choice." She hadn't said that when she was free, when she knew the Population Police were going to be out of power. She'd said it when Luke had broken into her house, when she had every reason to believe she could be killed for her defiance.

And he remembered the last time he'd ever seen Jen, the night before she left for her rally. The last words she'd spoken to him were, "We can hope"—even though she had to have known then that her rally was doomed.

Even when I was in hiding, I made my own choices, Jen

seemed to be whispering in his head. *I chose the possibility of freedom over everything else.*

Luke thought about how Oscar seemed to care about power more than anything else.

He thought about his friends and what they valued. Trey believed in words and books and knowledge. Nina savored memories of her grandmother and the "aunties" who had raised her, and she tried to live up to their vision of her. Percy, Matthias, and Alia, three kids Luke had met through Nina, believed in God and in trying to do the right thing.

And me, what do I believe in? What do I care about the most?

He'd come such a long way from being the little kid cowering in the attic, when he thought it didn't matter what he cared about, what he believed in, what he wanted.

But I've had to make choices all along. At home, at Hendricks School, with the Grant family, when I was hiding out at Mr. Hendricks's house, when I was working undercover for the Population Police, in Chiutza . . .

He could imagine Jen goading him: *Enough with the reminiscing, Luke. Save the nostalgia for another time. Are you going to do this or not?*

He gave his answer out loud. "Jen, this is my decision, not yours. It's maybe the most important decision of my entire life. Let me think for a minute."

He walked over to the stable door and poked his head out, so he could see the vast crowd fanning out from the stage. It seemed bigger than ever. *How many of those people are already so dead-set against third children that they could never change their minds?* Luke wondered. *How many don't care one way or another? How many of them maybe . . . possibly . . . potentially . . . could be on my side?* It was like one of those tricky math problems he'd had to do back at Hendricks School, involving percentages and probability. He'd never been any good at that kind of math, and this time his life might depend on figuring the probability right.

What percentage of the crowd didn't boo third children last night? He wondered. He didn't know. He couldn't know. Math problems didn't allow for leaps of faith, but sometimes that's what you had to take in real life.

"Hope you're good at jumping," he muttered to Jenny, and went to get her saddle.

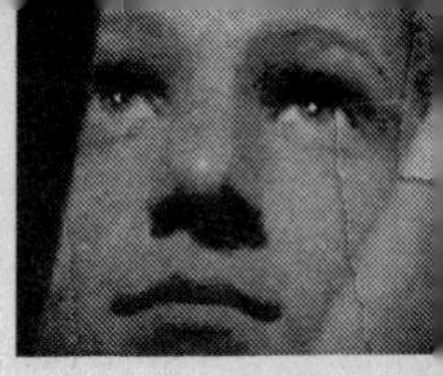

CHAPTER THIRTY-ONE

Luke sat atop Jenny's back, high off the ground. He'd never actually ridden a horse before, just cleaned out their stalls and groomed them and fed them and led them around. His imagination hadn't allowed for how wobbly and unsteady he'd feel on horseback, as if any minute now Jenny might simply dart out from underneath him and let him go crashing to the ground.

"You wouldn't do that to me, would you, girl?" Luke asked nervously.

It would help if he could hold on with both hands, but he'd gotten scared that the security guards would recognize him. So he had the quilt draped over his head, with his left hand clutching it tight at his throat. That left just his right hand for grasping the reins. He flicked them, the way he'd seen the Population Police officers do.

"Let's do this, okay?" he said, trying to sound authoritative and strong, as if it mattered that he could fool a horse.

Jenny glanced back at him doubtfully, then took a few halting steps forward. Maybe it did matter how forcefully he gave his commands.

"You're going to have to go faster than that," Luke said, and flicked the reins again.

This time Jenny took him seriously, and she lunged forward, out the stable door. It was all Luke could do to hang on. Making his plans, he'd imagined Jenny galloping gracefully across the lawn, the crowd parting easily before her, everyone struck dumb with awe. What actually happened was that he had to duck to keep from being knocked off by tree branches, and then he had to yank his leg away from someone who tried to grab him. And then it looked like Jenny's hooves were going to land right on top of a little girl, but the girl's mother snatched her away at the last minute. And everyone was screaming, screaming so loudly that it terrified Jenny and she raced through the crowd even faster, causing even more narrow misses.

And then, suddenly, it was time for the leap.

Jenny was a smart horse—she tried to veer to the side, alongside the stage, rather than make the dangerous jump. But Luke urged her onward. He let the quilt go flying off behind him, and he took hold of the reins with both hands, holding them firm and steady, not letting Jenny face any direction but straight ahead. She tensed her muscles and sprang up, and for one terrible moment Luke was certain that he'd slide off backward and land right at the feet of the line of security guards. He grabbed onto the horn of the saddle, and he must have pulled on the reins at the same time, because Jenny slid to a halt as soon as her hooves landed.

They were on the stage.

Luke was half in and half out of the saddle, and his feet got tangled up in the stirrups as he tried to climb down. He fell in a heap on the stage, his right shoulder landing first. By the time he managed to scramble to his feet, the newscaster Philip Twinings was right beside him, screaming at him.

"Young man, you've terrified the entire crowd with that beast! You have no right—"

Luke grabbed the microphone out of Philip's hands.

"But I had to show everyone—this is a Population Police horse. They had horses to ride for fun while everyone else was starving and desperate. That had nothing to do with third children. It wasn't third children's fault, and neither was anything else the Population Police did!"

Philip didn't grab the microphone back right away.

"Ah," he said thoughtfully. "You should have the right to say that, up on this stage, if that's what you believe. But there's a protocol that has to be followed. You have to sign up to speak, you have to talk to our screening committee and wait your turn and not just come barreling up here, endangering lives—"

"Your screening committee would never have let me come up here, if I asked permission," Luke interrupted. "Don't you see what's going on? Haven't you been listening?

It's all a setup, everybody saying the same thing. The only people allowed to talk now are the ones who will blame third children, not the Population Police. But it's all a lie. Third children didn't steal anyone's food. They didn't force the Population Police to beat anyone. Third children don't have any power at all."

"How do you know that?" Philip Twinings asked.

Luke didn't plan his answer. He was just desperate. He could feel his time on the stage slipping away, as Philip Twinings reached out for the microphone, as security guards rushed toward the stage stairs.

"Because I'm a third child," he said.

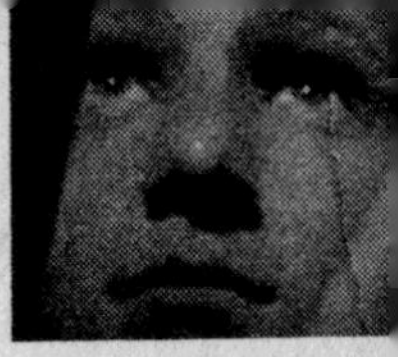

CHAPTER THIRTY-TWO

The crowd really did fall silent then. Luke thought that he could see thousands of faces with their jaws dropped, doing nothing but staring at him, Luke, now fully revealed. It was a scene straight out of his worst nightmares.

The crowd's reaction was so horrifying that it took Luke a few minutes to notice what the security guards at the front had done:

Every last one of them had pulled out a gun.

Luke froze, feeling strangely resigned. *So this is how it ends,* he thought. He was acutely aware of the sunshine streaming down on his head, the slight breeze ruffling his hair, the awful silence of the crowd.

And then Philip Twinings stepped in front of him, shielding Luke's body with his own.

"You will not shoot this boy," he thundered, his voice as powerful as a prophet's. "Or if you do, you will have to kill me first. And you will be destroying any chance our country has for a fresh start, any hope for an honest government. Put those guns away!"

Luke peeked out from behind Philip Twinings's back. The security guards seemed to be hesitating. Then one of the cameramen climbed down the stage stairs and stood right beside the line of guards, filming each one of them in turn.

"Yes!" Philip Twinings shouted. "If you shoot, every person in this country will know who you are, what you've done. No more secrecy! No more hiding our crimes!"

One by one, the security guards began tucking their guns away, holding their hands up, palms out, as if to prove their innocence. The cameraman stayed close by, continuing to guard the guards.

Behind them there was a tussle in the crowd, and a woman stood up, clutching the quilt that Luke had dropped.

"I made this quilt!" she was shouting. "It was mine."

The word "stolen" flew through the crowd, and whispers of "of course the boy took it" turned into louder opinions: "What do you expect from a third child?" "It's just like all the other speakers said . . ."

"No, no!" The woman was screaming now. She fought her way through the crowd toward the stage. When she got to the line of security guards, they shrugged nervously, glanced at the cameraman, and let her through. With difficulty, she climbed up the front of the stage and took a microphone from an unattended stand.

"My name is Aileen Mootispaw," she said, "and I can tell you that the boy did not steal this quilt. It was a gift to him, from my father, when my father thought he was about to die. When he thought he could not possibly do enough to make up for informing on a third child to get food for his own family—food the Population Police never delivered."

Luke realized with a jolt that she was talking about Eli—Eli, who had handed the quilt to him, murmuring, "This is Aileen's handiwork . . ."

"My father did not die," Aileen continued. "When we saw the boy with this quilt on television two nights ago, my father sent me here to find him, to make sure he was safe. So I speak on behalf of my father and myself and our entire village—and in memory of the third child we betrayed. Let this boy tell his story!"

"I—" Philip Twinings began to say.

But there were others streaming up toward the stage now, chanting, "Let him speak! Let him speak!" Luke thought he recognized Ricky and Don and a few others who had been in the truck with him when he'd ridden to the celebration of the Population Police's overthrow the first night. One of the women chanting reminded him of the old woman in Chiutza who'd told him, "I have a choice." But the others were strangers, people he could have sworn he'd never seen before in his life.

Luke had no idea what percentage of the crowd was standing at the front, chanting in his support. He had no idea what the ratio was between the chanters and the ones who stood stony-faced and angry behind them. He couldn't calculate the probability that he could win over anyone else.

But he thought he had a chance.

Philip Twinings was holding up his hand, trying to regain control of the crowd.

"This is indeed irregular," he murmured, when he once again had everyone's attention. "I wanted this to go in an orderly fashion, to encourage openness and people speaking without fear. But—" He glanced toward the table where the three members of the screening committee were all glaring at him. "I fear the rules of orderliness became too restrictive. I was tricked once before, when we first faced the famines and droughts, when the government began to control my news station's coverage—to prevent panic, they said . . ." He seemed to get lost temporarily in his memories of the past. Then he shook his head, his old eyes clearing.

"We will let the young man speak," he said.

Luke stepped forward to the edge of the stage. The waiting crowd was still terrifying to look at, and his mouth went dry.

"I'm just a kid," he said, trying to make excuses for himself, to explain why he wasn't going to do a very good job, why he wasn't the best person to be standing there defending the cause of third children. But then he saw how some of the people in the crowd looked more thoughtful when he said that.

"Really," he went on, "I'm not any different from any other kid. I like football and baseball and just about any kind of game. I don't like sitting still, indoors. Third children aren't beasts or monsters or devils. We're just . . . born third."

Talking wasn't so bad as long as Luke kept going. He felt the crowd's eyes boring into him only when he paused to take a breath, to get his thoughts together. He gulped and forced himself to continue.

"When I was born, my parents thought I was a miracle, a special blessing. A gift. But from the very beginning they had to hide me. They thought the Population Law would eventually be repealed. They never dreamed that I'd never be able to come out of hiding without a fake I.D. . . ."

To explain his fake I.D., Luke had to tell about Jen and her rally, about how he'd been in agony wondering what had happened to her. He told about meeting Jen's father and going to Hendricks School, and how bewildered he'd felt there, how dangerous the school had been. He told how the Grant family had wanted to use him, and how that was when he met Oscar.

At first, Luke was careful not to say anything that would get anybody else in trouble. He didn't tell his parents' names; he was careful to refer to Mr. Talbot only as "Jen's dad." Mr. and Mrs. Grant were dead now, and Smits Grant was living under a different identity, so it didn't matter what he said about them. But when he got to talking about Oscar, he hesitated.

Oscar is acting like he's going to be our country's next leader, Luke thought. *People ought to know what they're getting.*

"And Smits's bodyguard was Oscar Wydell," Luke said.

The whole crowd seemed to gasp. Too late, Luke thought that it might be dangerous to mention Oscar. Maybe his name would be the cue for Luke to be yanked off the stage. Philip moved over closer to Luke, but he just stood there protectively, and muttered, "Go on."

Luke tried to be fair talking about Oscar. He said that Oscar had protected him, some of the time. He said that Oscar had thought Luke was too timid and cowardly. But he also said that Oscar had manipulated people; Oscar hadn't cared who got hurt as long as he came out ahead.

"You're a brave young man," Philip murmured beside Luke. "You're the first person who's been willing to provide us any insight into this mysterious man."

Luke winced at that, but he couldn't stop talking now.

He told about his friends Trey and Nina and Matthias, and what their lives had been like in hiding. He told how he'd been kept in a holding camp when the Population Police took over the entire government, and how Trey and Mark had managed to rescue him. He told how he and his friends had decided to join the Population Police, to sabotage it from inside.

"So yes, we were fighting the Population Police. But we weren't doing that just to be selfish, to hurt everyone else. We tried to give food away. We wanted *everyone* to be free," he said. He hesitated. "It's hard to know how everything fits together. Maybe we were even working with Oscar Wydell some of the time. Maybe we were on the same side."

Some in the crowd mumbled angrily at that. Luke swallowed hard, momentarily lost. *I'm wrong,* he thought. *Oscar wasn't involved in our plans. He wouldn't have been willing to do the little jobs, take the small steps toward freedom. Oscar just came forward to take the credit when none of us did. When I was scared and wanted to hide again. . . .*

The crowd's murmurings grew louder. The rising tide of sound threatened to overwhelm Luke.

Philip Twinings put his hand on Luke's arm.

"Keep going," he said softly in Luke's ear. "What happened next?"

Luke shook his head, to clear it.

"Chiutza," he said.

And then he was able to talk about the woman who'd refused the Population Police orders, saying, "I have a choice." He told about how he'd run away rather than be forced to shoot her. He told about the fighting in Chiutza, and the fields and houses that the government had forced Eli and his friends to abandon. He started to tell how Eli had sent him away when the Population Police arrived, but Aileen interrupted him.

"No, no, that wasn't the Population Police coming back that night—that was all of us who'd been taken away by the Population Police. We'd gotten free and we were bringing food back to our village. Eli tried to send someone after you, to get you to come back," Aileen said, "but no one could find you."

"Oh," Luke said, blinking. He remembered how the wind had seemed to call, *Lu-uke. Lu-uke,* and how he'd thought it was a trick. "I was so used to being in danger, to having to be scared. I never thought that it might be . . . safe . . . to come out of hiding."

Something about the way he said that made the crowd laugh, but it was friendly laughter. He hoped.

"So," Luke said, "then I saw the news on TV in another village, and I came here. And everybody else was so happy, but I just couldn't be sure. . . ."

He told about seeing the signs in the secret room, and overhearing the conversation between Oscar and Aldous Krakenaur.

"No! That's not true!" someone yelled from the crowd. "Oscar Wydell is not a—a collaborator!"

"Shut up!" someone else yelled. "Aren't the signs evidence enough?"

And then lots of people in the crowd began shouting at each other and arguing. Some of the security guards at the front started to reach for their guns, but then they glanced at the camera and shrugged, as if to say, *It's not our problem what people say. Who can stop them?*

Luke took a step back from the microphone. He shook his head dizzily, trying to understand what was happening. He'd lost the crowd's attention. But he couldn't tell if that was because most of them believed him or because most of them were on Oscar's side. He could do his trick of closing one eye and then the other, and the sides seemed to jump back and forth.

Oscar's side is winning . . . no, mine . . . no, Oscar's . . .

"Ah, the lovely sounds of free speech," Philip Twinings said beside him.

"They're just arguing," Luke said, still dazed. "The whole crowd is fighting."

"Yes, but they're using words, not bullets," Philip said. "So much better than the stupefied silence of the past few hours. Or the past thirteen years."

"You opposed the Population Police, then," Luke said. "Why didn't you say so? Why did you let all those speakers blame third children, all morning long?"

Philip Twinings sighed. His ancient eyes seemed to hold decades' worth of pain.

"I did sabotage the microphone, last night," he said. "But this morning—I was afraid. Things seemed to have changed. I was in exile for a very long time. I didn't want to go back. And—I was only one person."

"Sometimes one person is enough," Luke said.

"Yes," Philip said. "And sometimes it takes a kid to show adults the truth."

Luke started to tell Philip, "You did help me—you made sure I got a chance to talk. You risked your life too." But he broke off because the crowd's uproar had reached a fever pitch. A group of men seemed to have come to a conclusion.

"We'll just get Oscar out here! He'll tell you!" Luke heard one of them shout.

"You do that! I want to hear what he has to say for himself!" someone else hollered back.

Luke watched the men rushing back toward the Population Police headquarters.

"Perhaps you should leave, young man," Philip said softly. "For your own safety."

"Are you leaving?" Luke asked.

"No. Of course not."

"Neither am I," Luke said.

He remembered way back in the fall, after the Grants had died, how he'd longed for a day of truth, when he and his friends could stand up proud and tell the whole world their true names, their true stories. He hadn't revealed his name, but he'd told everything else. No matter what happened, he was glad he'd done that. He had no intention of hiding again, of cowering back in the stables, dreading every approaching footstep. He was done with that life.

Jenny whinnied behind him, and he went to stand beside her and stroke her mane.

"It's all right, girl," he said. "Don't be afraid. I'm not afraid anymore."

He understood now how the old woman in Chiutza had been able to look so peaceful facing the gun; how Jen could have gone off so bravely to her rally. They'd made their choices. They'd been free.

And now so was he.

The mob that had rushed into the Population Police headquarters came rushing back out.

"He's gone!" the men were yelling. "Oscar ran away!"

Out of the corner of Luke's eye, he saw the three former Population Police officials scrambling away from the screening committee table. He saw them slipping into the shadows, sneaking out the back door. He saw the security guards walking away from their posts. He saw the Oscar supporters in the crowd shrugging or slumping—giving up.

It was over.

CHAPTER THIRTY-THREE

Luke's friends showed up that afternoon, while he was with a crowd pulling down the signs opposing third children. The words THEIR FAULT came off in his hands, and he was tearing them to bits when he heard a familiar voice behind him.

"Need some help with that?"

He whirled around to find Nina, Trey, and Mr. Talbot standing there, and they ran to him, hugging and exclaiming.

"Where were you guys?" he asked. "I kept looking for you—"

"When the Population Police fell, we all went to Mr. Hendricks's house. We kept thinking you'd join us there. We didn't think there was anything else to worry about," Nina said apologetically.

"But we turned on the TV this morning and heard the speeches and saw the signs—we came as fast as we could," Mr. Talbot said. "We just didn't know what we could do."

"Then we turned on the radio in the car and heard this

crazy kid telling his life story," Trey said. "You were great, Lee—you really were."

The fake name sounded more jarring than ever, after everything Luke had been through. He looked around at the people tearing down the signs; at the noisy, still-arguing crowd; at Philip and Simone and Tucker standing before the cameras interviewing people again.

"I'm free now," he said. "You can call me Luke."

He remembered how baffled he'd been all along, trying to understand freedom. In the beginning, all he'd wanted was a chance to run across his family's front yard or ride in the back of the pickup truck to town, the way his brothers did. He'd seen how the Chiutzans acted like freedom just meant getting to shoot anyone they wanted to shoot; how Eli and the others in his village thought they were free because they were ready to die. He'd watched the people celebrating at Population Police headquarters as if freedom were just a matter of getting free food.

But he understood now that freedom was more than that. In one sense, he'd been free all along.

"Is it safe to talk like that?" Mr. Talbot asked, glancing around anxiously. "Have you heard—did they catch Aldous Krakenaur?"

"No," Luke said. "He escaped with Oscar."

"Then he could come back," Trey said. "He could get the Population Police back together, consolidate his power again—"

"We're making sure that doesn't happen," Luke said. He

pointed at a bunch of people gathered around a table someone had pulled out onto the grass. "That group is talking about writing a new constitution to guarantee everyone's rights." He pointed to another table at the other end of the yard. "They're talking about how to distribute food fairly until the next harvest." He watched a man and two women setting up another table nearby. "I'm not sure what they're going to talk about at that table, but *this* is our new government. The people."

His friends stared at him in amazement.

"Good grief," Mr. Talbot said. "We've gone from ideologues to idealists."

"Don't you think it will work?" Luke asked.

Mr. Talbot peered around at the crowd. Luke could see how he might be doubtful: Most of the people at the tables were pretty young; they were dressed in ragged clothes and had shaggy hair. They didn't look like a government.

But Mr. Talbot grinned.

"This is the best chance we have," he said. "Maybe I'll go check out that constitution they're working on . . ."

He wandered off, and Nina and Trey settled in with Luke, pulling down the signs. The adhesive Oscar's supporters had used was very strong; it was difficult erasing every trace of every hateful word. But Luke and his friends were persistent, working side by side.

"So I'm the only one who didn't go to Mr. Hendricks's house?" Luke asked.

"All our friends are there—and lots of other third children who didn't have anywhere else to go. Your brother's there too," Nina said. "His leg's still in bad shape, but Mr. Talbot said he was in charge of protecting the younger children if anything happened."

If anything happened . . . Luke shivered, thinking about how easily Oscar's plans could have succeeded. How easily, even now, the new freedom could be stifled if people didn't guard it carefully, didn't use it wisely.

"Mark's disappointed that he never got to come back here and work undercover," Nina said. "He says he missed all the fun."

"Fun?" Luke snorted. "Right. I would have traded places with him in a heartbeat. He could have ridden Jenny for me. He could have stood up on that stage."

"No," Nina said, "he couldn't have. It had to be one of us."

A third child, she meant. In the end, only a third child could have stopped Oscar.

"Weren't you scared?" Trey asked, scrubbing at the shadowy backing left by the sign. "Admitting you were a third child in front of that huge crowd—in front of the whole country, really—"

"Of course I was scared," Luke said. "But I had to do it, you know?"

He looked at his two friends, and he knew they understood. They had also taken some terrifying chances. They had also risked their lives for freedom. It made the job of tearing down signs seem simple by comparison. Luke wondered if this was how it would be for the rest of their lives: that any other dangers or challenges they might face would pale in comparison to what they'd survived as kids.

We'll have a "rest of our lives" now, Luke thought, surprising himself. *We will.* He'd never dared to think that far ahead before. But now he gazed back out over the vast crowd again, and he could almost see everything he wanted to happen, stretching out far into the future.

He could see his family rushing through the crowd to find him—having seen him on TV, they wouldn't be able to sit at home, waiting, anymore. And instead of whisking him off home to try to keep him safe, they would decide to stay and help. He could see his dad telling the new government how to deal with farmers, his mother telling them about factory workers.

He could see Matthew getting to raise hogs again. He could see himself playing football with Mark again—Mark's leg finally fully healed—and maybe with Jen's older brothers, Brownley and Buellton, as well, when they came back safely to the Talbots' house.

He could see old, abandoned fields reclaimed, resplendent with new crops. He could see roads and bridges and houses all over the country repaired and rebuilt, all the warped framework set right, all the broken windows replaced.

He could see Oscar Wydell and Aldous Krakenaur and all the other Population Police officials caught and tried and sentenced, so none of them could haunt his nightmares ever again.

He could see Mr. Hendricks and Mr. and Mrs. Talbot working in the new government. Maybe one of them would be the new leader—a leader chosen by the people, not just forced into office through brute strength. Maybe someday he or Nina or Trey might even campaign to be elected, and then lead the country that had once said they had no right to exist.

He could see Nina taking care of her grandmother and aunties the way they'd once taken care of her. He could see Trey becoming a college professor someday, and Matthias becoming a minister, and Percy an engineer, and Alia, little Alia—well, maybe someday she'd be a doctor like Mrs. Talbot.

He could see all the timid, odd third children he'd known at Hendricks School getting a chance to lead ordinary lives—or maybe extraordinary lives. Maybe one of them would become a great inventor or a great writer or a great philosopher or . . . who could say what they might be capable of now?

He could see Smits reclaiming Population Police headquarters as the Grant house again, turning it into a home for children who'd lost their families. And he could see the boy on crutches, the one who'd been beaten by the Population Police, helping out.

He could see himself as a grown man with a farm of his own, married with children of his own—maybe two, maybe three, maybe more. He would take his wife and children and go back for Sunday dinners with Mother and

Dad and Matthew's family and Mark's family. And they'd all sit at the same table, all together.

He could see himself and his friends gathering each year at a memorial for Jen and all the other third children who'd died in the rally. He could see himself staying longer than everyone else, bending down over the memorial so he could touch the cold stone and whisper to the ghostly memory of a girl who would never grow up, who had sacrificed everything for her beliefs: *Jen, we did it. Everyone's free now.*

He didn't know if any of those things would really happen.

But they were all possible now.

Here's a look at Margaret Peterson Haddix's book *Found*, which launches her new series, The Missing.

PROLOGUE

It wasn't there. Then it was.

Later, that was how Angela DuPre would describe the airplane—over and over, to one investigator after another—until she was told never to speak of it again.

But when she first saw the plane that night, she wasn't thinking about mysteries or secrets. She was wondering how many mistakes she could make without getting fired, how many questions she dared ask before her supervisor, Monique, would explode, "That's it! You're too stupid to work at Sky Trails Air! Get out of here!" Angela had used a Post-it note to write down the code for standby passengers who'd received a seat assignment at the last minute, and she'd stuck it to her computer screen. She knew she had. But somehow, between the flight arriving from Saint Louis and the one leaving for Chicago, the Post-it had vanished. Any minute now, she thought, some standby passenger would show up at the counter asking for a boarding pass, and Angela would be forced to turn to Monique once more and mumble, "Uh, what was that code again?" And then Monique, who had perfect hair and perfect nails and a perfect tan and had probably been born knowing all the Sky Trails codes, would grit her teeth and narrow her eyes and repeat the code in that slow fake-patient voice she'd been using with Angela all night, the voice that said behind the words, *I know you're severely mentally challenged, so I will try not to speak faster than one word per minute, but you have to realize, this is a real strain for me because I am so vastly superior. . . .*

Angela was not severely mentally challenged. She'd done fine in school and at the Sky Trails orientation. It was just, this was her first actual day on the job, and Monique had been nasty from the very start. Every one of Monique's frowns and glares and insinuations kept making Angela feel more panicky and stupid.

Sighing, Angela glanced up. She needed a break from staring at the computer screen longing for a lost Post-it. She peered out at the passengers crowding the terminal: tired-looking families sprawled in seats, dark-suited businessmen sprinting down the aisle. Which one of them would be the standby flier who'd rush up to the counter and ruin Angela's life? Generally speaking, Angela had always liked people; she wasn't used to seeing them as threats. She forced her gaze beyond the clumps of passengers, to the huge plate glass window on the other side of the aisle. It was getting dark out, and Angela could see the runway lights twinkling in the distance.

Runway, runaway, she thought vaguely. And then—had she blinked?—suddenly the lights were gone. No, she corrected herself, *blocked.* Suddenly there was an airplane between Angela and the runway lights, an airplane rolling rapidly toward the terminal.

Angela gasped.

"What now?" Monique snarled, her voice thick with exasperation.

"That plane," Angela said. "At gate 2B. I thought it—" What was she supposed to say? *Wasn't there? Appeared out of thin air?*"—I thought it was going too fast and might run into the building," she finished in a rush, because suddenly that had seemed true too. She watched as the plane pulled to a stop, neatly aligned with the jetway. "But it . . . didn't. No worries."

Monique whirled on Angela.

"Never," she began, in a hushed voice full of suppressed rage, "never, ever, ever say anything like that. Weren't you paying attention in orientation? Never say you think a plane is going to crash. Never say a plane could crash. Never even use the word *crash*. Do you understand?"

"Okay," Angela whispered. "Sorry."

But some small rebellious part of her brain was thinking, *I didn't use the word* crash. *Weren't you paying attention to me? And if a plane really was going to run into the building, wouldn't Sky Trails want its employees to warn people, to get them out of the way?*

Just as rebelliously, Angela kept watching the plane parked at 2B, instead of bending her head back down to concentrate on her computer.

"Um, Monique?" she said after a few moments. "Should one of us go over there and help the passengers unload—er, I mean—deplane?" She was proud of herself for remembering to use the official airline-sanctioned word for unloading.

Beside her, Monique rolled her eyes.

"The gate agents responsible for 2B," she said in a tight voice, "will handle deplaning there."

Angela glanced at the 2B counter, which was silent and dark and completely unattended. There wasn't even a message scrolling across the LCD sign behind the counter to indicate that the plane had arrived or where it'd come from.

"Nobody's there," Angela said stubbornly.

Frowning, Monique finally glanced up.

"Great. Just great," she muttered. "I always have to fix everyone else's mistakes." She began stabbing her perfectly manicured nails at her computer keyboard. Then she stopped, mid-stab. "Wait—that can't be right."

"What is it?" Angela asked.

Monique was shaking her head.

"Must be pilot error," she said, grimacing in disgust. "Some yahoo pulled up to the wrong gate. There's not supposed to be anyone at that gate until the Cleveland flight at nine thirty."

Angela considered telling Monique that if Sky Trails had banned *crash* from their employees' vocabulary, that maybe passengers should be protected from hearing *pilot error* as well. But Monique was already grabbing the telephone, barking out orders.

"Yeah, Bob, major screwup," she was saying. "You've got to get someone over here. . . . No, I don't know which gate it was supposed to go to. How would I know? Do you think I'm clairvoyant? . . . No, I can't see the numbers on the plane. Don't you know it's dark out?"

With her free hand, Monique was gesturing frantically at Angela.

"At least go open the door!" she hissed.

"You mean . . ."

"The door to the jetway!" Monique said, pointing. Angela hoped that some of the contempt on Monique's face was intended for Bob, not just her. Angela imagined meeting Bob someday, sharing a laugh at Monique's expense. Still, dutifully, she walked over to the 2B waiting area and pulled open the door to the hallway that led down to the plane.

Nobody came out.

Angela picked a piece of lint off her blue skirt and then stood at attention, her back perfectly straight, just like in the training videos. Maybe she couldn't keep track of standby codes, but she was capable of standing up straight.

Still, nobody appeared.

Angela began to feel foolish, standing so alertly by an open door that no one was using. She bent her head and peeked down the jetway—it was deserted and turned at such an angle that she couldn't see all the way down to the plane, to see if anyone had opened the door to the jet yet. She backed up a little and peered out the window, straight down to the cockpit of the plane. The cockpit was dark, its windows blank, and that struck Angela as odd. She'd been on the job for only five hours, and she'd been a little distracted. But she was pretty sure that when planes landed, the pilots stayed in the cockpit for a while filling out paperwork or something. She thought that they at least waited until all the passengers were off before they turned out the cockpit lights.

Angela peeked down the empty jetway once more and went back to Monique.

"Of course I'm sure there's a plane at that gate! I can see it with my own eyes!" Monique was practically screaming into the phone. She shook her head at Angela, and for the first time it was almost in a companionable way, as if to say, *At least you know there's a plane there! Unlike the other morons I have to deal with!* Monique cupped her hand over the receiver and fumed to Angela, "The incompetence around here is unbelievable! The control tower says that plane never landed, never showed up on the radar. The Sky Trails dispatcher says we're not missing a plane—everything that was supposed to land in the past hour pulled up to the right gate, and all the other planes due to arrive within the next hour or so are accounted for. How could so many people just lose a plane?"

Or, how could we find it? Angela thought. The whole situation was beginning to seem strange to her, otherworldly. But maybe that was just a function of being new to the job, of having spent so much time concentrating on the computer and being yelled at by Monique. Maybe airports lost and found planes all the time, and that was just one of those things nobody had mentioned in the Sky Trails orientation.

"Did, uh, anybody try to contact the pilot?" Angela asked cautiously.

"Of course!" Monique said. "But there's no answer. He must be on the wrong frequency."

Angela thought of the dark cockpit, the way she hadn't been able to see through the windows. She decided not to mention this.

"Should I go back and wait? . . ."

Monique nodded fiercely and went back to yelling into the phone: "What do you mean, this isn't your responsibility? It's not my responsibility either!"

Angela was glad to put a wide aisle and two waiting areas between herself and Monique again. She went back to the jetway door by gate 2B. The sloped hallway leading down to the plane was still empty, and the colorful travel posters lining the walls—"Sky Trails! Your ticket to the world!"—seemed jarringly bright. Angela stepped into the jetway.

I'll just go down far enough to see if the jet door is open, she told herself. *It may be a violation of protocol, but Monique won't notice, not when she's busy yelling at everyone else in the airport. . . .*

At the bend in the ramp, Angela looked around the corner. She had a limited view, but caught a quick glimpse of a flight attendants' little galley, with neatly stowed drink carts. Obviously, the jet door was standing wide open. She started to turn around, already beginning to debate with herself about whether she should report this information to Monique. Then she heard—what? A whimper? A cry?

Angela couldn't exactly identify the sound, but it was enough to pull her on down the jetway.

New Sky Trails employee saves passenger on first day on job, she thought to herself, imagining the praise and congratulations—and maybe the raise—she'd be sure to receive if what she was visualizing was real. She'd learned CPR in the orientation session. She knew basic first aid. She knew where every emergency phone in the airport was located. She started walking faster, then running.

On the side of the jet, she was surprised to see a strange insignia: TACHYON TRAVEL, it said, some airline Angela had never heard of. Was that a private charter company maybe? And then, while she was staring at it, the words suddenly changed into the familiar wing-in-the-clouds symbol of Sky Trails.

Angela blinked.

That couldn't have happened, she told herself. *It was just an optical illusion, just because I was running, just because I'm worried about whoever made that cry or whimper. . . .*

Angela stepped onto the plane. She turned her head

first to the left, looking into the cockpit. Its door also stood open, but the small space was empty, the instruments dark.

"Hello?" Angela called, looking to the right now, expecting to see some flight attendant with perfectly applied makeup—or maybe some flight attendant and a pilot bent over a prone passenger, maybe an old man suddenly struck down by a heart attack or a stroke. Or, at the very least, passengers crowding the aisle, clutching laptops and stuffed animals brought from faraway grandparents' homes, overtired toddlers crying, fragile old women calling out to taller men, "Could you pull my luggage down from the overhead for me? It's that red suitcase over there. . . ."

But the aisle of this airplane was as empty and silent as its cockpit. Angela could see all the way to the back of the plane, and not a single person stood in her view, not a single voice answered her.

Only then did Angela drop her gaze to the passenger seats. They stretched back twelve rows, with two seats per row on the left side of the aisle and one each on the right. She stepped forward, peering at all of them. Thirty-six seats on this plane, and every single one of them was full.

Each seat contained a baby.